Wrench's Salvation

Wolfsbane Ridge MC

Book 4

Author Marissa Ann

Credits:
Cover Design by: Francessca PR & Designs
Editor: Rachel Goldman
Blurb: Melissa Mitchell

ASIN:
ISBN-13: 978-1-7365798-8-6

Chapter 1
Wrench

I'm glad to be back home. Really, I am. But I'm still pissed off about getting discharged because of a fucked up shoulder injury. Like, what the fuck? My shoulder wouldn't have stopped me from being able to do the fucking job.

I had tried to appeal the decision with my superiors but they wouldn't go against doctor's orders. It fucking sucks, but that's the military for you.

When I first got home, everyone tried to steer clear of any conversations that would bring up my time with the military, as if afraid of pissing me off. At least until I set them all straight.

I'm not fucked in the head because of anything that happened while in the service. I'm fucked in the head because they had pushed me out before I was ready to leave.

The night I came back home, I met a beautiful blonde that is new to White Summer. She owns Hays Den, the little work out studio where the other girls take self-defense classes.

Hayden had intrigued me from that very first night. She's the reason I always volunteer to keep an eye on the girls when they go into town. Especially on the days they have class.

Like the creeper I am, I stand in the back of the room with my eyes trained on her every move. She acts as if she doesn't notice, but I know better.

I see the way she peers at me from the corner of her eye whenever she thinks I'm not watching. But I'm always watching. She's so damn beautiful she literally takes my breath away.

I'm so lost in this creepy new hobby of mine that I don't notice anything but her. Until I feel a small tug on my cut. Looking down, I see the beautiful little girl I recognize to be Hayden's daughter.

"Hello, little one." I smile down at her, waiting to see what she will say. I know from previous visits that she's an outspoken little girl and I know I won't have long to wait.

"You're the only man in here," she whispers, her eyes wide and serious. "Why?"

I drop to my knee and meet her gaze. "I'm making sure no one messes with the women while they work."

She considers that a moment before asking, "Like a bodyguard?"

I grin. "Yep. Like a bodyguard."

"Can you be my bodyguard?" There's something in her eyes that I can't quite put my finger on.

"Why would someone as cute as you need a bodyguard?" I tap her on the nose with a smile.

"Hanley! You're supposed to be in the office." We both look up as her mother reaches us. "I'm so sorry if she was bothering you." Hayden scoops the child into her arms.

"She wasn't bothering me," I assure her. "We were having a very serious conversation about bodyguards."

She chuckles a little at that. "Why would you two be talking about bodyguards?"

"I told her I was the women's bodyguard, and she asked if I could be hers as well." Something I can't quite figure out flashes in her eyes and her smile fades.

"Well, the girls are all done for the day. So, I guess we will see you next time." Spinning on her heel, she hurries away before I can say another word.

"What was that about?" Mina asks, approaching me with the others, their workout bags all slung over their shoulders.

"No idea." I frown and glance in the direction Hayden had disappeared and then offer to carry a few of their bags.

Why had she reacted that way when she found out what Hanley and I had been talking about?

Hayden

Back in my office, I set Hanley down in front of the toys she'd left scattered in one corner.

The door pops open behind me and I spin around to see Austin, one of my employees and closest friends rushing in. "Hey, are you okay? I saw you talking to Wrench then running to your office as if the fires of hell were after you."

"Haven't I asked you to knock before just walking on in here? And I wasn't running." I roll my eyes and scowl as he chuckles at my expense.

"Oh, you were definitely running. He doesn't bite, you know. Unless, of course, you want him to. Do you want him to?" He perches on the edge of my desk with a smile on his face, as if he already knows the answer.

I groan. "Don't you have other things to do? Like taking inventory in the back room or something?"

"Does everything have to be about working with you? When was the last time you went on a date?"

I lift my nose in the air and take a seat at my desk, directing my gaze on my computer screen. "Why do you care?"

"I'm fairly sure you haven't gone out with a man since the jack-hole we don't talk about."

My eyes snap to him, poised and ready to bite his head off for even remotely mentioning *him*. "I go out to eat with *you* all the time."

"That's not a date. We tried that whole dating thing back in high school, remember? One kiss and we knew we weren't meant to be. Was like kissing my sister or something." He wrinkles his nose. "Gross."

I reach out and shove his shoulder. "It wasn't that bad. Besides, you don't even have a sister."

"Well, if I did, kissing her would be just like that. No sparks. At all. And I can't be hanging out with you all the time. I love you, but I need to go out with the guys. Maybe get a little action. Find my perfect woman."

I snort out a laugh. "That'll never happen. Your perfect woman doesn't exist. Unless, of course, you're hoping for a Stepford Wife.

Austin grins and shrugs. "You never know, Hayhay. She may be out there, just waiting for me to come along and sweep her off her perfect little feet."

I smirk, rolling my eyes at the very idea of it. "I hope she's the total opposite of what you want, and I also hope she gives you hell every step of the way."

Austin pushes himself off my desk and narrows his eyes in my direction. "That hurts. Seriously, you're not my best friend anymore."

"Guess that means you won't be there for supper then?" I call after him as he strides out of my office.

His head pops back around my door. "What are you cooking?"

"Spaghetti and meatballs with a salad on the side."

"I'll be there at eight."

He disappears once more, ignoring my quiet chuckle.

My gaze drifts over to Hanley, where she sits, completely engrossed in whatever she's watching on her tablet.

Then I think back to what Wrench had said about bodyguards and Hanley had asked him to be hers. Does she remember what we had gone through with her father?

I refuse to call him her dad. That kind of title is to be earned, not freely given.

Two years in the state prison of West Virginia is all he got for what he had done to me. That two years is almost up though, and soon, he'll be getting out. As part of his parole, he's not supposed to leave the state and I can only hope that will keep us safe from him a little longer.

The phone rings, pulling me from my thoughts. Mina's name flashes on the screen.

I stab the talk button with one finger and put the phone to my ear. "Hey, girl. You forget something?"

"Actually, I did," Mina says. "I wanted to invite you to our family cookout on Saturday. Hanley will have a lot of kids to play with and it'll give you time to hang with us girls. What do you say?"

I purse my lips and consider that for a moment. "Umm, well, I'm not sure. I need to check my schedule first."

Just then, Austin walks back into my office. "Check your schedule for what?"

"Mina invited Hanley and me for a cookout on Saturday."

Shaking his head, Austin reaches over and presses the button on the phone base, switching it over to speaker mode.

"She will be there," he says, ignoring my wide eyes. "She never schedules things on Saturdays."

I glare daggers at his big, stupid face, but he pays me no mind.

"You're welcome too, Austin," Mina says with the hint of a smile in her voice.

Austin smirks. "I will be there," he replies. "And I will make sure Hayden is there, too. On time."

"Perfect. Saturday at noon," Mina says. "That's when the guys actually start up the grills. See you all then."

We say our goodbyes and I wait to hear the click of the line disconnecting. Narrowing my eyes to sharp slits, I glare vicious daggers at Austin.

"What?" he asks, his eyes wide with fake innocence.

"Don't what me," I snap. "What if I didn't want to go?"

Austin rolls his eyes. "You know damn well you want to go, and we both know why. Wrench."

"You don't know anything," I huff.

"I know you better than you'd like to admit."

"I don't really like you, you know," I lie.

"I know you love me, so you'll get over it."

His laughter echoes through the open door as he exits the room and makes his way down   the   hall.

Wrench

Mina had invited Hayden and her daughter to the cookout on Saturday, and when she'd accepted, I had released a breath I hadn't even realized I'd been holding.

I haven't gotten excited about anything in a very long time, but anything to do with that woman excites the ever loving hell out of me. The closest thing I'd ever felt was when I'd been overseas, waiting for the enemy to pop his head up over the sand dunes.

"You stare at the door any harder and it's likely to explode into flames. Looking for someone?" Timber plops down next to me on the bench.

"I don't know what you mean." I turn, watching the kids playing around the tree with the tire swing hanging from it.

"Yeah, okay. Whatever you say." He leans back and changes the subject. "You get to that Super Glide this week?"

"Purring like a kitten now," I reply, happy for the distraction. "Tell the guy to just bring it in next time, instead of trying to fix it himself."

Timber shrugs. "You know as well as I do, most of these guys like to act like mechanics, even though they don't know shit about how the bike works."

Just then, his phone dings with an alert. I watch as he pulls it from his pocket and looks down at the screen. And then his face changes.

"Something wrong, Prez?"

Timber shakes his head and stuffs the phone back into his pocket. "Not sure, yet. But no worries today. Today is the day to relax and enjoy family. How is your mom, by the way?"

I shrug. "I haven't called her since I've been home. She wrote me a letter when I was overseas, gushing about how she'd reconnected with some guy she'd been pining over for the last twenty years or so."

Timber raises a brow. "You should call her. Invite them out for a visit."

I look back toward the kids, ready to change this subject, too. "Yeah, maybe."

"What the hell are you mad at her for, anyway? Do you even know?"

I frown. "I'm not mad. Not really. And anyway, what the hell does it matter to you?"

"It matters because you have a damn good mom. She's always there for you, even when you don't want her to be. I'd give anything to have mine back. You're a lucky bastard to have her and you don't even care." Timber shakes his head, then gets up and walks towards the back door.

This has been a never-ending argument between the two of us. And I know he's right, even though I'll never admit to shit.

To be honest, I don't actually know what the hell I'm pissed off about with my mom. And that just pisses me off even more.

Hayden

"Yay, you're here!" Mina cries as we walk into the giant kitchen.

I'd been here before, but this time there were way more people. Most of the adults are out back playing and running around with the kids.

Hanley tugs on the bottom of my shirt. "Can I go play?"

"The kids are out in the back," Mina says. "But I make no promises of her staying clean. Not with all those other wild hoodlums running around out there."

I grin at Mina's description of the kids I hear screaming from the yard, and look down at my daughter. "Yes, but please try to not get too dirty." I may as well be speaking in Chinese, though.

"I won't," she hollers back, already running out the door.

Bella laughs from her place at the bar. "Where's Austin? Wasn't he coming with you?"

"Out front, talking to one of the guys. I think his name was Bear. He's the one that told me I could find you girls here."

Miranda holds up a bottle and motions to the blender she's been pouring stuff into. "We are making margaritas. You want one? It will help us drown out all the screaming kids."

"Sounds great, I say with a smile. "Who are all the kids, anyway? I don't recognize some of these people."

"Some of them are extended family members of the guys. Cousins and such," Mina says as she pours herself some tea. That's one downside to pregnancy, I suppose. You can't enjoy a drink with the girls.

"The family dynamics around here will confuse you." Miranda shakes her head.

I tip my head to the side. "What do you mean?"

"You may be introduced to someone who says they are a cousin, but that doesn't necessarily mean a cousin by DNA. Kind of the same way the guys in our club see each other as brothers. Guys from another club can be seen as cousins."

"Seems complicated. Does that make all the women your cousins?"

Mina raises a brow. "That would be a firm no. I don't like people that easily."

"That's for sure," Bella says with a laugh, then ducks as Mina throws a strawberry at her.

Miranda finishes up the margaritas and hands them out, one by one. "Come on," she says, picking up a drink of her own. "Let's go sit on the benches under the tree."

Outside, my eyes search out my daughter, and I instantly spot her sitting on a bench, under the tree, right next to Wrench. My cheeks flush from just how perfect they look together.

"Looks like Hanley's made a friend," Mina says, sitting on one of the bench seats under another tree.

I stare at the pair together for a moment. "I'd hate for her to bother him. Maybe I should go get her."

Bella waves her hand dismissively. "She's fine. Wrench is a great guy and really loves kids."

I watch them for another second and then decide to let it go. For now. But my attention is only partially on the conversation as the girls tell me all about Fiona, the sister of one of the club members, Blood.

Apparently she had made quite a name for herself as a tattoo artist, and the club had bought her a building where she could open her new studio, here at home.

"The Poison Pen is coming right along," Miranda informs us all. "The grand opening is scheduled to happen in two months. Which means she's counting on us to help with paint colors and ideas for how she wants it to look. You should help, Hayden."

"Yeah, I mean if you guys want some help, just let me know." I glance back over at my daughter, who is still sitting and talking with Wrench.

I watch as the pair stand up and he takes her hand, leading her over to the tables where the food is all laid out.

I can't sit back and watch for another second. Excusing myself from my group of friends, I stand and head toward them.

"Hello," I greet, reaching the table and smiling down at my girl.

"Hey, mommy!" Hanley cries, her excitement contagious. "Want a hamburger? Mr. Wrench says he fixes the bestest ones in Montana."

"Oh, I would love one, but I can fix my own." I press my lips together and smile at Wrench.

"I'll fix you one too. I don't mind." He lifts the corner of his mouth in a slight grin, making him appear even sexier. *Good God.*

"Thank you," I say a few minutes later, when he hands me a plate.

"No problem. Let's go sit under the tree and eat." Although he directs his comment to my daughter, he looks back to be sure I'm following along behind. I take a seat once we reach the bench they'd been sitting on before.

"I see Mina and the other girls have already made you one of them." His eyes are one me, watching me, as if I'm the only woman he sees. It's a little distracting, I have to admit, but I like it.

I force that thought away and shrug. "I guess so. They're all really sweet. They're the only friends I've made since moving here."

He nods. "How do you like our little town so far?"

"It's beautiful here. It's one of the reasons I picked this area."

Wrench pauses. "What's the other reason?"

I really don't want to answer that question. It's too personal. So, I just look back at him instead, until he gives a slight nod of understanding and goes back to his burger.

"I'm done now. Can I go play?" Hanley asks, breaking the silence as she stands up.

"Go throw your plate away."

She kisses my cheek, then grabs her paper plate and takes off at a run.

"Sweet little girl," Wrench murmurs as we watch her running around with the other kids. "Good manners, too."

I flush. "Thank you. Sometimes, I'm afraid I'll mess it all up, but she's a good kid."

"I'm sure all parents feel that way sometimes. But I can tell she'll be an amazing woman. Just like her mother."

My eyes shoot to him and goosebumps pop up all over my skin, despite the heat outside. The way he's looking at me makes my breath catch in my throat. *Oh boy, I think I'm in trouble.*

Chapter 2
Wrench

After spending most of the afternoon on Saturday either talking to Hayden or watching her from afar, I feel like I'm going through withdrawals by the time Monday comes around.

I never had brought up what Hanley had said to me before we had eaten our lunch, but I can't get it out of my mind.

Mina and the girls aren't taking Hayden's class today, but I need to see her.

Hanley had left her teddy bear behind on Saturday, giving me the perfect excuse to pop over to the studio. That little girl is scared, and I plan to make sure she is safe. After all, she paid me a nickel to be her bodyguard. I've already been hired for the job.

"Wrench," Austin says as I step through the front door. "How's it going, man?"

"Pretty good." I lift the teddy bear. "Hanley left this at the clubhouse on the weekend. Plus, it's a beautiful day. Thought I'd see if Hanley would like to go to the park. Her mom too, if she wants."

Austin grins. "Smooth. They're in her office. And, if she tries to say she doesn't have time, you remind her that her schedule is clear for the next three hours."

I chuckle. Looks like her friend is on my side, anyway. "Thanks man. I appreciate it."

He nods. "Just be good to her, or I'll have to kill you."

I know he'd said it as a joke, but I also didn't miss the hint of warning in his tone. Too bad for him, I could take him out with one hand tied behind my back. But it's good to know he's protective of her. Bear had told me that Austin and Hayden have been friends since high school.

In fact, he probably knows the whole story about Hanley, and why the little girl is so afraid. I may have to get some of those answers from him later. But first, I hope Hayden will answer them herself.

Hayden

I'm just finishing up last month's sales reports when my office door opens. Looking up, I expect to see Austin. Instead, my heart skips a couple of beats to find Wrench smiling back at me.

"Mr. Wrench!" Hanley yells, jumping up from where she'd been playing and dashing toward him.

"Hey, kiddo. You forgot this, so I thought I would bring it by." Dropping down to her level, he pulls her teddy bear from behind his back.

Hanley grins and hugs the bear to her chest. "Thank you, Mr. Wrench. I thought I lost him forever!"

"Thanks for bringing him back," I say, watching as Hanley runs over to her little table and places her bear in a little chair. "She was pretty upset."

Wrench moves forward and takes a seat in the chair across from my desk. I had figured he'd leave now that he'd returned Hanley's beloved toy, but clearly that's not happening.

"No problem," he replies, staring at me in silence for so long, I start to fidget. "I was actually wondering if the two of you wanted to go to the park. Maybe get an ice cream?"

His smile was already devastating, but coupled with those blue-green eyes, it melts my insides.

"I don't know," I say, my mind racing to come up with a believable excuse.

Wrench holds up a hand. "Before you start objecting, I already know you have nothing going on for the next couple of hours. Austin told me so."

I freeze. "Oh, he did, did he? Sounds to me like Austin needs to be finding himself a new job, because as of now, he's officially fired." I cross my arms over my chest, ready to rip my so-called best friend a new one. He may be a muscled-up tough guy, but I can still kick his ass.

Wrench chuckles. "Come on. It's a nice day. Gives her a little time outside. Plus, there'll be ice cream. Who doesn't love ice cream?"

Thirty minutes later, we're sitting side-by-side, eating ice cream cones and watching Hanley play on the slides with several other girls she'd introduced herself to as soon as we'd gotten here.

"She makes friends so easily. Wish I had been more like her when I was in school," I muse.

He regards me for a moment, before saying, "School wasn't easy for you?"

I shake my head. "Not at all. It was a little easier in high school, though, after Austin and I became friends. I guess having the football star on your side is the only way to make it through school."

"It's good to have someone who will kick some ass for you. I never could stomach bullies. Were you bullied a lot?"

I shrug. "I was a foster child. Grew up in a home full of other foster kids. The parents only cared about the money they got for us each month."

Wrench shakes his head slowly. "I'm sorry you went through that. What about your biological parents? Where were they?"

"There was no father listed on my birth certificate, and I was told that my mother died giving birth to me. She was only fifteen. Her parents refused to take me in, so I went into the system." I force my voice to stay even and unaffected, as if the trauma of my childhood was no big deal.

"That's fucked," Wrench says with annoyance. "Your grandparents are assholes."

I shrug. "They were well off and didn't want the embarrassment, I guess. Unfortunately for them, I still wound up with their last name."

"Lynn is your ex-husband's name then?"

"Yes. My maiden name is Hayden LaRue." I pause to see if he recognizes the last name.

His brows lift in surprise. "LaRue? From West Virginia?"

"Yep," I reply, popping the p on the end of that affirmation.

He considers that for a moment. "Well, look at you now. You own your own business and you're raising a little one by yourself. I would say you're doing pretty damn well in life without those assholes." His giant hand covers mine and it's all I can do to not tear up.

No one other than Austin has ever told me I'm doing a good job. While I try my best to not let my past hurt so much, it still does to this day. It's important to me that I don't let that touch Hanley, though.

We watch Hanley play in silence, but I keep glancing down at where his hand still covers mine. It's playing all kinds of havoc in my body, and my mind. If the butterflies in my belly flutter any harder, I'm likely to explode. I'm lost in thoughts of his hands until he breaks our silence.

"I know it's not really my business, but I have to ask. Did something happen to Hanley? She's said a few things that make it seem as if she's truly scared of something."

Pulling my hand from his, I stare straight ahead, my mind switching into overdrive as I try to think of how to answer that without saying too much.

I keep my voice cool as I ask, "Why do you ask?"

He leans forward and pins me in place with his gaze. "She asked me to be her bodyguard and even paid me for the service."

I frown. "Paid you? How?"

"She paid me a nickel." He chuckles at that and I can't help but smile at the innocence in my daughter's action.

But then I remember what he's asking and I know I have to get out of here. Fast.

"While I appreciate your concern, you were right. Our problems aren't your business." I stand and call out for Hanley before turning to face him again. "Thank you for the ice cream. We had best get back to the studio."

Wrench

Real smooth, jackass. I make my way back to the clubhouse, the conversation with Hayden playing over and over again in my mind. Of course she had bolted. I'd pried. But I couldn't help it. I feel drawn to her and to Hanley.

Hayden may be hesitant to share her story with me, but I know Hanley is scared and that just doesn't sit right with me. I know Timber often has Snake look into the people the clubs have any dealings with, so even though it may overstep my bounds with Hayden, I decide to pay him a visit.

"Hey, Prez. Got a minute?" I ask, poking my head into his office at the shop.

"Sure. Everything going okay in the shop?" He leans back in his chair as I take the seat across from him.

"Yeah, no problems there. I'm already starting on the new carburetor for that trike. But that wasn't what I wanted to ask." I lean forward, holding his stare. "I was wondering if you had Snake do a full background on Hayden?"

Timber raises a single brow. "Of course I did. But I'm more curious why you're so interested?"

I don't hold back. If I'm going to get this information from him, he needs to know there's a good reason for me to know.

"I think they're running from something. Possibly someone."

Timber studies me for several beats, his fingers tented in front of his face. "Explain. Start from the beginning."

"Last week, when I took the girls to class, Hanley asked me why I was there. I told her I was a bodyguard. Then on Saturday at the cookout, she paid me a nickel to be her bodyguard too."

"You get what you pay for," Timber chuckles as he turns and digs into his file cabinet. Paper rustles as he rifles through the stacks of files and finally pulls out the one he's looking for.

I watch as he opens it up on the desk and stares down at it for a moment, his eyes growing stormy. "Here it is. Ex-husband, Henry Lynn. Currently serving time in West Virginia's state prison. Convicted of assault, battery and false imprisonment nearly two years ago. He's scheduled for release soon, if he's not out already."

I grit my teeth. "Who did he assault?"

"I think you already know the answer to that," he answers, his expression grave. "I'm thinking, if Hanley knows any of this, or even heard whispered conversations about it; this could be why she's afraid. Especially if she was a witness to any of it." He shakes his head, frustrated. "I'll get Snake to pull the bastard's arrest reports and anything else he can find. See if we can get a better picture of what went on."

I feel like I've been punched in the gut, images flashing in my mind of Hayden being hurt by the man who'd vowed to love and protect her, all while her daughter watches. "Thanks, Prez."

Anger bubbles inside my veins. That fucker better pray he doesn't get near Hayden or Hanley. It will be the last move he ever makes.

Chapter 3
Hayden

I'm just finishing up some laundry when there's a knock at my front door. Austin had come earlier in the day to take her Hanley to stay the night with his mom, and besides him, I never get visitors.

Through the tiny window of the door, I can clearly see Wrench on the porch. My heart speeds up just at the sight of him. And then I remember I'm completely bare of makeup, with my hair piled on top of my head in a bun.

"Hi," he says as I open the door.

I flush. "Hi, yourself." I glance around behind him, wondering if perhaps he'd brought Mina or one of the others over for a visit, but I don't see anyone besides him. "What are you doing here?"

"Was wondering if you two would like to grab a bite to eat down at Bella's Brew. Some of the guys will be there with their ladies."

I shake my head, relaxing just a little. "That sounds like fun, but Hanley isn't here. She went to stay the night with Austin's mom. She takes her several times a month, so I can have a little time to myself. According to her, all mom's need it and she won't take no for an answer."

"Remarkable woman," he says with a smirk. "So would you like to come along?"

I glance down at my frumpy outfit. "I'm not exactly dressed to go anywhere."

"We have time," he says, his eyes traveling along my body. I feel them like fingertips as he takes me in from the top of my head to the tips of my toes. And then his lips twist into a smile that makes my heart race inside my chest. "Go. Get dressed."

I swallow, ignoring my own quick breathing and suddenly hardened nipples, before turning away and motioning him to follow me inside.

"Make yourself at home," I say, pointing to the couch and then heading down the hall to my bedroom. "I won't be too long."

Shutting my door, I dash to my closet, frantically searching for a clean pair of jeans and a shirt. My makeup, since I wear so little, shouldn't take me long to apply. I rarely wear any these days. *Should I text Austin and tell him I'm actually going on a date? Oh shit. Is this a date? I should probably make sure my legs are shaved. Just in case.*

You know what? I'm going to be me and he can just deal with it. Hairy legs or not.

Wrench

A few hours later, we're sitting at one of a group of tables, along with the rest of the guys and their old ladies. The girls are laughing and making plans for the upcoming opening of the Poison Pen. It's coming up quickly and there is still a ton of work to be done.

I watch Hayden when she doesn't know it, admiring the way her entire face lights up when she's laughing. She's so damn beautiful. Especially when she's laughing. How could any man have her—have a taste of perfection—and fucking it all up by being cruel to her?

She has caught me watching her several times, though, and every single time, her cheeks flush the prettiest shade of pink, causing the front of my jeans to grow tighter and tighter.

It's extremely clear that I want this woman on a physical level, but I also want to get to know her. Every single thing about her is attractive to me. I've never felt drawn to a woman like this before. It's all so new to me.

"We should all go to Black Cat on Friday night," Mina says. "There's a live band playing and we haven't all been out like that in a while. Would be fun."

Bella nods. "It would be nice to see Sara. She hasn't been by the coffee shop in quite a while. At least not when I was there."

"She's been taking classes at the local college," Timber says. "Wants to become a nurse. Paul said she hardly gets any sleep between the classes and helping him at the bar. If you girls want to go Friday, we can do that."

"What about you, Hayden? Come with us." Mina extends the invitation, but I can only stare at Hayden, praying she agrees. I need more time with her outside of seeing her at the studio.

Hayden nibbles on her lower lip for a moment, considering. "Maybe. I'll have to see if Austin's mom will keep Hanley for me."

The conversation turns then, and the girls chat amongst themselves, excited as they make plans for our night out. They even discuss what they are going to wear. I don't hear what Hayden says, but I would be more than appreciative to see Hayden in another pair of jeans. The woman has an amazing ass. I'd love to see it ripple after a nice hard spank from my hand.

I breathe, closing my eyes and trying to focus on something else. *Down, boy*. The last thing I need is to be sitting here with a giant hard-on, surrounded by my buddies.

Hayden

Back at my house, I can literally feel Wrench's eyes on my ass as he walks me to my door. I unlock the dead bolts and then turn to face him. The look of hunger in his eyes freezes me in place.

"Would you like to come in?" I ask in a whisper.

Without a word, he crowds in and his lips claim mine, setting my skin on fire. I can't suppress the moan that escapes as I get my very first taste of him. I wrap my arms around his neck and at the same time, he lifts me. His large hands grip my ass as I wrap my legs around his waist.

He breaks the kiss, his gaze boring into mine as he carries me through the door. He heads straight inside and down the hallway, looking into each room, looking for mine.

Once inside, he slowly lowers me to my feet, next to my bed. I reach out for the button on his jeans, but his hands cover mine to stop me.

"I just want to touch you, Hayden. Will you let me?" His voice is thick with a whisper as he licks the shell of my ear with the tip of his tongue, sending shivers shooting throughout my already hypersensitive body. "I need you to answer with your words, baby."

"Yes," I breathe, moaning as he slowly undresses me.

Getting me down to my red bra and g-string, he steps back, looking at me with a fire I can only hope is an indication for what's to come.

"Fuck," he growls. "You are so fucking beautiful. I want to fuck you while you wear that. Just pull that little string to the side and glide myself into that wet pussy. It's wet for me, isn't it?" His hands glide along my sides until he is kneeling before me. I can feel his breath through the lacy material at my clit.

My heart is about to beat its way right out of my chest, and I don't realize he's still waiting for an answer until I feel a slight sting to the bottom of my ass from his hand. Instead of feeling hurt, I feel myself throbbing with want.

"You like that," he murmurs, then lands a spank to the other side. "Lay back on the bed for me, beautiful."

He helps me to sit down and lower myself until my back lands on the soft, pillowy mattress, my legs hanging off the side, right in front of him. His wide shoulders hold my knees apart, giving him access to my center.

His tongue reaches out and licks up the center of my G-string. I moan again, feeling wanton with need.

"Mmm. You taste as good as I thought you would."

Lifting my head, I look down at him, breathing hard. He slowly pushes the material of my panties to the side and with his burning eyes on mine, he slowly lowers himself and plunges his tongue into my center. I throw my head back in both shock and pleasure. I've never felt anything so glorious in my life. Now is probably not a good time to tell him that nobody has ever had their mouth down there before.

That's the last full thought I have before his mouth sucks at my clit hard, not letting go until I am catapulted over the edge into the most mind-blowing orgasm I have ever experienced.

He keeps licking and kissing until I am spent. His kisses then travel up my body, all the way to my mouth. I taste myself on his lips, and it is a turn on I never expected to have.

I try to reach for his jeans, and yet again, he stops me.

"What about you?" I ask in a small voice, afraid I did not please him.

"Not tonight. Tonight I just had to taste you. I've wanted to ever since I first laid eyes on you. It was the night I came home from the military, and you were snowed in with us at the clubhouse."

"Don't you want me in that way?" I ask, confused.

He says as he presses his hard cock into my center. "Does it *feel* like I don't want you in that way?"

I frown. "Then, why?"

"Maybe I'm not that type of guy. Maybe my big plan is to make you fall madly in love with me before letting you have my body." He grins, his eyes bright.

I snort and push at his shoulder slightly. "Be serious."

"I'm more serious than I've ever been," he says, pulling the covers up over our bodies, and then snuggling into my back. "Now go to sleep."

"Are you at least going to get down to your boxers to sleep? You're going to be uncomfortable."

"I'll be fine," he replies. "Besides, I don't want you taking advantage while I sleep."

"You sure are full of yourself."

"I know. Now go to sleep."

Within a few minutes his breathing evens out, and his body grows heavy with sleep against my back. Must be a military thing to be able to go to sleep so fast.

I'm not sure what makes him think he can make me fall in love with him. I'm a single mom struggling with a new business. *Why would a guy like him want someone like me, anyway?*

Wrench

I wake the next morning, pretty early like I always do, but to my surprise, I had slept through the night, not waking up from the persistent nightmares that never seem to go away. I had lost so many good men and every one of them haunts my dreams.

Mikey had become a really close friend while in the service. The day I got hurt, he died and I know I'm still alive today because of him.

His body had landed on mine when the bomb hit us, throwing me to the ground. The impact of both our bodies landing on the ground is how my shoulder had gotten too mangled to serve any longer.

I'd been so angry. I didn't care about my shoulder. All I really wanted to do was go back and shoot the hell out of more insurgents for losing my friends. They wouldn't allow it, though.

Shaking my head to clear those memories, I slip out of bed quietly, careful not to wake her. In the kitchen, I put on a pot of coffee and browse through her cupboards to see what I can fix for breakfast.

I'm just pulling the bacon out of the pan when she comes in from the hallway, her sleepy eyes blinking up at me with surprise.

"I thought you had left already," she says, taking a seat at the bar and smiling softly when I hand her a cup of coffee.

"Why would I leave without saying goodbye?" I frown, genuinely curious, but she just shrugs her shoulders.

I set a plate of eggs, bacon and toast in front of her, before getting one of my own and taking a seat next to her.

"What's your plans for today?"

"Austin usually brings Hanley home around seven on Sunday evenings, after his mom and her get home from church. Hanley loves going to church with her and playing with all the kids there."

I smile, then snag my chance to spend more time with her. "Then you're free to hang out with me today."

"You want me to spend the day with you?" Her eyes are wide with surprise.

"Of course I do," I say, nudging her shoulder gently with mine. "I told you I was going to make you fall in love with me."

"I thought that was just..."

"Me trying to get in your pants? Nope."

I pick up our empty plates, washing them in the sink before drying them with a towel and putting them away.

"I'm sorry," Hayden sighs. "I just don't have a very good track record with men. Most just want a good time and I tend to stay away from that. You seem to be an exception."

I smile at her words and stalk back towards her. She doesn't see me. Her eyes are still pointed down at the counter in front of her, so she jumps slightly, letting out a sexy squeak of surprise when I press my lips to her ear.

"An exception, huh? See? You're already falling head over heels for me." I kiss her ear and neck, reveling in her trembles as goosebumps pop up along her arms.

"What if you don't fall in love with me? What then?" she whispers.

"That'll never happen. My mom always said I would know within minutes. I thought she was nuts, but now, I'm thinking she knew exactly what she was talking about."

"I have a kid." She turns then, looking up at me with bright, vulnerable eyes.

"I know. And I love her already, but I plan on giving her a few siblings one day." I press between her legs, getting even closer to her. Thoughts of making more babies with her playing in my mind.

"Go get dressed for a ride on my bike," I say, pushing back from her before I end up taking her right there on the counter. "But pack your swimsuit."

Her cheeks are pink as she nods. "Okay."

Hayden

Several hours later, I'm lying next to the pool at the Wolfsbane Ridge Clubhouse with all the other girls.

"All the times I've been here, I never even knew this was here," I marvel. "I thought this building was just another shop with tools or something."

"Each time Timber finds out about another lot next to the clubhouse going up for sale, he buys it, then builds something new," Mina says from the lounger next to mine. "It's his dream for all the club members' houses to be built here, but he wants to be sure they have everything they could ever want first."

"Sounds like a cult," I say on a laugh, but only partly kidding.

"I guess it does," she chuckles. "Especially looking in from the outside. But a lot of these guys don't have homes of their own. That's why they started building the cabins. Then they realized they could build more and rent them out. That's how Wolf's Ridge got started."

Several families not related to the club rent cabins here on a yearly contract," Fiona says from my other side. "They like knowing the guys won't allow any craziness. There's several areas dedicated to just the kids and all of them are monitored with sound and motion activated cameras. Makes it the safest neighborhood around."

Bella sits up from her chair. "You rent a house on the other side of town, right?"

"Yes, on West Street."

"Do you let Hanley go outside to play over there?" Bella raises her brows, as if she already knows the answer.

I shake my head, knowing that my neighborhood isn't very good, when just the thought of letting my daughter out to play in our own backyard causes anxiety. "I see your point."

I sit, worrying for the next several minutes, afraid I've upset the friendships I've made with these wonderful women. I'm the only true outsider in our little group.

"Hey, you okay?" Miranda bumps my shoulder with hers.

"I hope I didn't make any of you mad by my comment."

"You didn't. You just don't know how everything works in the club. You'll learn as you go, just like I did." She smiles as she draws us back into the conversation the other girls are having.

"Those fucking frogs are the reason I had to work at the butcher. I've never thrown up more in my life." Fiona holds her hand to her mouth while looking a little green. "Think I lost a kidney down the toilet."

"Frogs? What are you guys talking about?" I ask, both confused and curious.

Bella rolls her eyes. "Technically, we can't talk about it."

"Club business," Mina adds, as if that explains it all.

I frown again, confused.

"Club business usually means something can't be discussed with anyone outside of the club. It can also mean that it is need to know information only. If the men say it to you, then you don't ask questions. Period. And no matter how much you ask, you won't get any answers." All the women roll their eyes, this time at Fiona's explanation.

"Sounds like a saying that needs to be struck from the dictionary to me." I say with wide eyes, and the women around me laugh.

"What are you women planning now?" Timber asks from the other side of the pool.

That just sets off another whole new round of laughter before Mina says, "Don't you wish you knew?"

Chapter 4
Wrench

Watching Hayden interact with the other women, I'm happy to see how welcoming they are to her. That's a good thing, considering I plan for her to be a part of it all.

Do I sound nuts?

Hell yes, I sound nuts. Either that woman is a witch that cast a spell on me or my mother hexed my ass with her talk of knowing within minutes if it was meant to be.

My mother. Timber was right. I should call her, but I'm not sure of what exactly to say. *Sorry for being a jackass son and being pissed at you for no apparent reason?* She'd probably laugh like hell in my ear, then ask how the weather is. My mom's a little wacky like that.

She was actually a pretty amazing mom when I was growing up. She was always there without judgment for me to talk to if I had a problem.

I know they say parents shouldn't be their kids' friend, but she was mine when I needed one. I remember the first time I ever smoked pot with my friends. They all went nuts when I picked up my phone to call my mom and tell her what I did.

She was cool about it, though. Told me she did not condone such behavior, but would never tell me flat out not to. She believed that's what made kids lie to their parents or hide stuff from them. She didn't want that with her kids.

Before she got off the phone, she told me to come up to the house and get something to eat because she knew I was hungry. I still laugh at that memory.

"You look different today. Smiling and shit," Blood says from beside me.

"I feel different today."

"Oh, shit," Bear mutters, looking around at Timber, Blade and Blood, and then gives a dramatic mock shiver. "He's been bitten by the same damn bug that got you three."

I laugh. "It'll get you one day too, Bear. Just wait and see."

"I hope like hell it doesn't. These three already act like pussies when their women are whining over even the smallest thing."

"I personally can't wait for the day it bites my ass," Snake murmurs into his beer.

"Why is that?" Timber asks.

"Because I like to bite back." His smile is almost evil as we all laugh out loud.

Hayden

We arrive back at my house a little before seven. As we are walking up my front steps, my neighbors choose that moment to fight with each other on their front lawn.

We both watch, shocked, as the couple scream profanities at each other. The woman is throwing his stuff out the front door and he's scrambling around, trying to pick it all up.

From what little I can gather from the names she keeps calling him, she caught him cheating again. After several minutes, the man finally gives up on grabbing all his things, climbs in his beat-up car and speeds away.

Wrench and I are still standing on the first step when the woman takes notice of us.

"What the fuck are you staring at?" she screams, before whipping around and storming back inside.

"Colorful neighborhood," Wrench says with a chuckle.

I laugh, shaking my head and heading to my own door. "Those two go at each other about every other day."

"Some people really shouldn't be together."

"I know too well how true that is," I say, digging out my key.

Just then, Austin's car pulls in the driveway. Hanley flies out of the front seat almost before the car is completely parked.

"Mr. Wrench!" she screams as she hurls her little body at him. *Is it bad that I love how easily he caught her in his arms?*

"Hey, sweetie. You have a good weekend?"

"Yeppers! We had a birthday party for a girl at church. I ate cake and ice cream." She smiles wide.

"Can I at least get a hello?" I ask her.

"Hello, Mommy. I missed you!" She holds her little arms out to hug me. When I lean in, she holds me close with one arm while she hugs Wrench with the other.

"My two favoritest peoples," she whispers.

"Hey, what am I? Chopped liver?" Austin holds his hand over his heart as if offended.

"My three favoritest peoples!" Hanley replies with a giggle. "Can I go watch cartoons?"

"Only for an hour, then you have to get ready for bed." Wrench puts her on the ground and she takes off, disappearing inside the house.

"Mom said she was an angel." Austin says, handing me Hanley's overnight bag.

I smile and roll my eyes. "She always says that."

"Well, she's a great kid. Don't know why you'd expect something different." Austin shrugs. "You two have a good day?"

"Yeah," Wrench says with a nod. "Spent the afternoon at the clubhouse pool. You should come sometime. Bear said you're into motorcycles."

"I used to own one. Been thinking about getting another one for a while now." Austin doesn't elaborate on why he no longer has the bike. I know, though. That crazy ass ex-wife of his. *Stupid bitch.*

"Well, come by the shop whenever you want and have a look around. We do some damn amazing custom rides."

Austin nods. "Will do. I got to run. Got a few more things to take care of around the house for mom."

"Guess she's getting you to finally fix that leak in the back bathroom?" I say with a laugh, and Austin rolls his eyes.

"Yes. I've already told her a hundred times, I am not a plumber. But does she listen? No."

"He acts all crazy, but he loves his momma. She's a good woman," I tell Wrench as we watch Austin climb into his car and drive away.

"It's good to be close to your mom." Wrench eyes glaze over with a faraway look.

"You close to yours?" I realize now just how little I know about him.

"Yes. No." He shakes his head. "Maybe?"

"Well, which is it?" I ask with a grin.

"A little bit of everything." He shrugs. "We used to be close, then—I don't know—I was just angry all the time. Took it out on her, I guess. I'm not exactly sure why. It's been a while since I've talked to her."

His admission saddens me. "Tomorrow is another day."

"Meaning?" He raises his questioning brow.

"Meaning she's still alive, and you should call her. You never know when any of us will leave this world. We should hold those we love as close to us as possible, for however long we have. Otherwise, you could wake up one day, find she has left this Earth, and realize you missed all those chances to make things right."

"Beautiful and smart." He tucks a lock of my hair behind my ear and leans in to kiss my lips. They tingle at the touch of his.

"Guess I should go help Hanley get ready for bed." I whisper, not yet ready to end the day.

He grins, something mischievous brewing in those eyes of his. "Text me when you go to bed."

"To tell you goodnight?"

"Something like that." He laughs, kissing my mouth again, before turning and heading for his motorcycle.

I stand on the porch, watching his taillights disappear around the corner before I head   inside.

Wrench

I've just dropped my ass into a seat at the bar in the clubhouse when one of the Yotes approaches, putting her nasty arms around me.

Yotes are what we call the club girls that hang around the club, offering "favors" to any of the guys that'll take them up on it.

Most of them are hoping one of the single guys will make them their old lady. What they don't seem to get though, is that will never happen when they are giving their snatch to any man around.

"Already told you, Sally, I'm not available." I remove her arm and toss it away from me.

"You don't have to be so rude. Besides, you need to loosen up a little. We could make each other feel so good." Her fake pouty lips disgust me.

There was a time when I would have taken her up on her offer. Back then, I often indulged myself with the free, unattached pussy around the clubhouse. I was younger then. Before the military.

These days, I prefer something more. A woman that hasn't had nearly every cock in the clubhouse pounding away at her. I shiver. *Thank God I'd always wrapped it up back then.*

"Go bother Fang," Timber snarls from behind her, causing her to jump.

She doesn't argue. Of course she doesn't. Timber is the President, and girls like her are only here because he allows it. Plus, his woman could beat her ass, even while pregnant.

"Thanks," I say. "I've told her multiple times to leave me the fuck alone. Including the night I found her naked in my bed. Mina had to find me some fresh sheets."

Timber chuckles. "Yeah, she told me about that. Mina's already had a talk with the Yotes about no meaning no."

"You'd think it'd an easy concept, considering most women chant, no means no."

"You'd think so. They mostly don't mean any harm. They're just hoping one of the brothers will put a ring on it." Timber shrugs.

"But they won't. Why would any man want a woman who gives it away so easily to multiple guys? Sometimes in the same week?"

"That's a double-edged sword," Timber says, nodding toward Dane, who is well known for spreading his love around. "I could ask why any woman would want a man that does the same?"

"You have a point." We clink our beers together and sit back, just watching the room.

We're watching Dane leave the room with two of the Yotes trailing after him, when my phone pings in my pocket.

Since Timber and a few of the other guys have been in relationships, a new rule was announced about the craziness that used to happen in this very room. No more sex in the middle of the room, or being naked at all.

Pulling my phone from my pocket, I see Hayden has finally sent a text to let me know she is heading to bed.

Hayden: Going to bed now. Had fun today. Thank you.

Me: You're welcome.

Hayden: Good Night!

Me: What are you wearing?

Hayden: Seriously?

Me: Yes.

Hayden: What's your real name?

Me: Seriously?

Hayden: Yes!

Me: Zack Fields

Hayden: Goodnight Zack.

Me: You're going to leave me wondering what you're wearing?

Hayden: Use your imagination ;)

I can't help but laugh at the little minx. She obviously doesn't believe that's exactly that what I will be imagining. Hell, I already am. I'm picturing her wearing a silk top that shows her nipples poking out, and a lacy pair of black thongs.

Fuck. I need to stop thinking about that while sitting in this room, surrounded by my brothers. I move around, trying to adjust myself without being noticed.

I'll file the thought away until I get to my room later tonight. I wonder if I could just sneak into her house and crawl into her bed...

Chapter 5
Hayden

Wrench and I have texted back and forth most of the week. He's even come by the studio to surprise Hanley and I with lunch in the park. He always takes time to play in the sand or on the swings with her and I have to admit, I kind of love that.

The two have a connection that worries me. What if this doesn't last? What happens when he decides he no longer wants to be in our lives? It'll break my daughter's heart. That's one reason I had sworn off dating. I didn't want her getting attached to someone who may not be around in a couple months.

He hasn't said anything more about making me fall in love with him. It may be too late, anyway. I'm kinda getting used to hearing from him all the time. My heart speeds up every night, anticipating his goodnight text. Each night, he asks me what I'm wearing, and each night, I tell him to use his imagination.

Now it's Friday though, and I'm getting ready for our night out at the Black Cat, to listen to the live band the girls had told me about. After a quick consult with Mina on what I should wear, I had opted for a pair of dark skinny jeans, a low-cut red top and knee-high black boots. Sexy, but casual, and comfortable enough to be on the back of Wrench's motorcycle.

The girls had enlightened me on that the other day. They'd told me that guys don't let just any girl ride on the back of their bike. That seat's reserved for their woman. Someone they're serious about. That bit of information gave me even more hope that Wrench isn't just stringing me along.

A knock comes at the door, and expecting it to be Wrench, I pull it open without looking.

My heart stutters. "Eric, what are you doing here?" My ex-brother-in-law is the last man I expect to see on my doorstep.

Eric was never around during my relationship with his brother. I had only ever met him twice. The first time was at our wedding. The second had been at the court proceedings. We had spoken a few times on the phone since then. He's a nice guy. The complete opposite of his stepbrother.

"I was in Bozeman for a meeting with a client. Figured since I was close, I'd come by to visit, before heading back to New York."

"Hanley isn't here right now," I say, pressing my lips together in an apologetic smile. "And I'm just getting ready to go out with some friends."

At that moment, an approaching motorcycle roars down the road, and we both watch as it pulls to a stop in my driveway.

Wrench

An unfamiliar, newer model rental car, complete with dark tinted windows, sits in Hayden's driveway. And at the front door, Hayden stands, watching me alongside an unfamiliar, well-dressed man. I can't help but narrow my eyes at how relaxed they seem to be with each other.

I look him over as I walk up to the porch. While the suit screams city boy, he's not a slender man. Broad shoulders suggest he works out regularly.

"Eric, this is Wrench, a friend of mine. Wrench, this is my ex-brother-in-law, Eric." Hayden makes the introductions as I reach out to shake his hand. Expecting to see derision on his face for being a biker, I'm surprised when he willingly shakes my hand with a smile.

"It's nice to meet you. I'm glad Hayden has found some new friends in the area." He turns back to Hayden. "I'm staying at a cabin on the other side of town for the next few days. It would be good to visit with you and Hanley before I leave, if that is alright?"

"You're staying at Wolf's Ridge?" I ask, making a note to check on the background information that would be in the clubhouse files. Timber checks out everyone thoroughly before renting out the cabins.

"I am. Although it was short notice, they were very accommodating. They even had a rental car waiting for me at the airport. I wish other places had such good customer service."

"We aim to please." I smile at the praise for my club, pointing to the emblem on my cut.

"Ah, your club owns the cabins, then? The woman that helped me was Mina. Very sweet woman."

"I don't know about sweet, but I'll let the Prez know you thought so of his wife." I chuckle at his description of Mina. I'm not saying she isn't sweet, but that girl can be downright ruthless when the need arises.

"I'm sorry we already had plans for tonight," Hayden tells him.

"He could go with us." I throw out the invitation, surprising both of them and myself. "He can follow us out there."

"I wouldn't want to intrude." His eyes dart between us.

"No intrusion at all. It's just a local bar we all go to. There's a live band tonight. It'll give you a chance to talk with Hayden." I was really hoping I wouldn't have to share Hayden too much tonight, but the manners my mom instilled in me insist on inviting him along.

"Sounds like fun. I rarely have time for that these days."

Hayden

Once inside Black Cat Bar and Grill, Wrench takes care of introducing Eric to everyone. Paul Blackcat, the owner, had reserved several tables for our group, in a spot where we could still see the stage without the music overpowering our conversations.

"So, what kind of work do you do, Eric?" Wrench asks from beside me.

"I'm a corporate lawyer, licensed in all fifty states. I cater to some of the most elite corporations in America."

"Sounds like too much work to me," Fang comments.

"Everything sounds like too much work to you," Dane drawls. That's why you were sleeping through the frog fiasco." Laughter erupts around the table.

"Why aren't some of you bitches dancing?" Fiona demands, walking up to the table. She then stops dead in her tracks when her eyes look next to me, recognition registering on her face. "Eric Dixon! What are you doing here? And with my family, no less?" Everyone at the table looks between the pair in surprise.

"Fiona! I didn't realize this was where you were from. I had heard you moved back home, but wasn't certain where that was." Eric smiles.

"You two know each other?" Blood asks from his side of the table.

"Yes. Fiona did some tattoo work for me. I have an idea about expanding though, whenever you can fit me in and my schedule allows it." Eric looks to Fiona for an answer.

"How about I call you as soon as the new shop is open? They're currently renovating it but it'll still be quite a few months."

"No problem. Just let me know and we'll work out something. Besides, it'll also be an excuse to come out to see my niece again."

We spend the next few hours listening to the music and enjoying the good food that Paul Blackcat brings out to our table.

I even get to slow dance with Wrench a few times. His body against mine makes me feel like I'm about to go up in flames. I've never felt like this with anyone before, not even my ex-husband. It feels wonderful and frightening all at once.

I'm lost in thought until I notice about five more guys walking up to our table. I remember seeing them around the clubhouse when I was snowed in there, although I hadn't been introduced.

"Who are they?" I whisper to Fiona.

"The big, older guy in the front is Butcher. He's a sweetheart. Behind him is Gear and Sprocket. They are identical twins, but nothing alike at all. Torque is the one wearing the sunglasses indoors, as if the light is too bright, but really it's because women are drawn to his eyes, and he hates the attention. And Jet is the one behind him. He's the one that looks like he's ready to leave although they just got here." Fiona laughs into her beer.

"Why does he hate the attention his eyes get him?" I ask, genuinely curious.

"Because right now, with the sunglasses on, he looks like any other guy sitting here, right?"

I nod.

"Wait until you see him without them. The man literally looks like a God come to life. He's the kind that inspires those Adonis statues. Women flock to him like moths to a flame. Most men would love it, but Torque hates it."

Wrench

With Hayden occupied by Fiona, I take the opportunity to talk with Eric, hoping he can elaborate a little more about Hayden's past with his brother.

"I was surprised to see you," I admit. "I figured her ex-husband's family wouldn't want anything else to do with Hayden, considering the circumstances."

"Her ex-husband is my stepbrother, but we've never been close. I only ever met Hayden a few times, including the day of the trial. My father and I had no clue what had been going on between them. If we had, we would have intervened."

"After the trial, I've stayed in touch with her. I want to make sure she and my niece have everything they need. At least, as much as she allows me to help, anyway." He raises his eyebrows. "That girl's as stubborn as they come."

I grin. "Sounds about right."

"The first time I met her was at the wedding. She was already pregnant with Hanley, and just starting to show. Looking back now, there was a problem with Henry even back then. My father and I had found her alone, crying in a backroom he had just walked out of. We had assumed it was pre-wedding nerves."

He shakes his head sadly. "Now we think it was something else. It wasn't until the trial when we learned what he had done to both Hayden and Hanley."

A hard ball forms deep inside my gut. "I thought it was only Hayden he assaulted."

"He didn't hurt Hanley physically, but definitely hurt her emotionally. Probably hurt her a great deal. He beat Hayden unconscious in front of her, then put Hanley into a trunk with a padlock. Luckily, he left before doing anything else."

"That's when Austin went to the house. He hadn't heard from Hayden after multiple texts and calls. When she didn't answer the door, he used the key she'd given him for emergencies. He called 911 when he found her in the bedroom in a pool of her own blood. It took even longer for them to find Hanley in the trunk down in the basement."

"Fucking hell," I grit out.

"I'd say that sums up what those two have been through perfectly."

We sit silently for several minutes after that. I watch Hayden talking with Fiona and the others. She's so beautiful and full of life. I can't imagine anyone wanting to ever hurt her.

Eric leans over and catches my eye. "Please take good care of them. They deserve everything good in life."

Trying to convey the sincerity of my words, I hold his eyes steady with my own. "I promise you, they will be cherished and loved for the rest of their life."

"That's all my father and I could ask. If you ever need anything—if they need anything—we are only a phone call away. There's nothing we would deny them. Those girls are family."

Sincerity burns in his eyes, but so does sadness. Maybe it's regret for what had happened. But he can rest assured, nothing like that will ever happen to my girls, ever again.

Chapter 6
Hayden

The next couple of weeks fly by. Every waking moment of my life seems to be completely filled with Wrench. I could be in the middle of teaching a class and I'd look up, and there he'd be, propped against a wall, a sexy-ass grin on his face.

Hanley had caught on to the fact that we were closer than friends, but she didn't seem to mind. She ate up the attention he gave to her. I noticed how it never mattered what he was doing—even if he was in the middle of something—when Hanley asked a question, Wrench stopped whatever it was, and answered her with a smile on his face. I am falling for him.

He spent most evenings at our house for supper before leaving to go back to the clubhouse. He never failed to message me before going to sleep, though. On the weekends, when Hanley was gone, he stayed the night in my bed.

In all that time, I never gave a single thought to the girls that were always hanging around the club. Mina had told me once a while back about them. She said everyone called them "yotes".

Tonight, however, as I watch a few of these girls prancing around in extremely revealing clothes, I wonder just how many of them Wrench has been with.

The club is having a party to celebrate a few of the newest members getting their patch. Ringo and Goose were introduced to me when we'd walked in. Both seemed nice enough, though I certainly wouldn't want them pissed off at me. They have a look about them that sends an automatic shiver down your spine.

Wrench was adamant we needed to be here, but now I'm thinking I should have just stayed home. A few times now, I have seen one girl trying to catch his eye. He's ignored it so far, but I'm not sure if I'll be able to if it continues. My blood feels as if it's coming to a boil as my jealousy grows, and that's pissing me off even more.

Since when am I a jealous person?

"You look ready to kill. You okay?" Mina leans over and whispers.

"I'm just realizing that I'm a truly jealous woman, and it pisses me the hell off," I grumble and she just smiles.

"Don't worry. He has nothing to do with any of them. Not even when you aren't around. At least, not since he's been back from the service. I'm not sure how he was before shipping out."

"That makes it a little better, but all bets are off if I catch her trying to touch him."

Mina throws her head back and laughs.

Wrench looks over at me with a smile, and I hope he didn't hear our conversation.

Some men don't like jealous women. I try to force myself to relax as I smile back at him.

"You ready to get out of here?" Wrench leans in to ask.

"Absolutely." I smile again, but this time with relief.

After saying our goodbyes to everyone, we finally make it out of the door and to the bike.

Wrapping my arms around his waist as we take off into the street, I can't help but relax into his broad, muscled back. He smells like leather and sunshine. It's becoming my favorite smell.

Wrench

"What do you want to do tonight?" I ask as we walk into her house.

Hanley is with Austin's mom again, until tomorrow morning. I miss her when she's not with us. I've never really given much thought to having kids of my own, but Hanley is so close to my heart, she already feels like mine.

"How about we order pizza and watch a movie on Netflix? I want a shower first though."

Her shower comment has me instantly hard although she hasn't yet looked at me.

Moving closer, I wrap my arms around her from behind and whisper into her ear, "Let's shower then." I watch as goosebumps pop up along her shoulders.

Grabbing her hand, I lead her to the master bath. Once there, I turn the water on, making sure it is just right before I turn to her with a smile.

Slowly, I reach for her shirt and lift it over her head, kissing the newly exposed skin as I go. Once her bra is free, revealing her perky nipples, I latch onto one, sucking hard, enjoying her sexy moan.

"Fucking beautiful," I whisper, releasing her nipple with a pop.

I drop to my knees, slowly sliding her panties down her thighs, never taking my eyes from her glistening center.

I lean forward and press my tongue against slit, unable to wait another second for a taste of her.

"Oh fuck," she moans, grabbing my head and trying to hold me in place.

"Oh no. You won't be coming on anything but my hard cock." I stand up, pressing my hardness against her, and point to the shower. "Get in. I'll be right behind you."

I help her into the shower, then strip my own clothes off and follow her inside. My cock stands straight out in front of me, hard as a brick.

Pulling her back to my front, I grab the soap and glide it over her silky smooth skin. I take my time, washing every curve of her body. Its absolute torture, but I want her more than ready for me.

"Please, Zack," she moans, as I drag my fingers along her slick core.

"You ready for me, baby?" I slide my cock along her ass, then down between her legs until the tip drags against her clit, and she coats me with her wetness. Slowly, I rock back and forth hitting her clit each time. "Tell me. I need to hear you say it."

"Yes! Fuck yes!" She writhes, pushing back into me, desperate for more.

I place a hand beneath her thigh, lifting her leg and lining the tip of my cock with her center. Slowly, I push inside her sweet, silky heat. We both moan until I am fully seated inside of her.

Hayden places her hands on the shower wall in front of her as I slowly ease out, then back in again.

"You feel so fucking good," I growl, setting her foot on the side of the tub so that I can use that hand to reach her nub.

"Faster. Fuck me faster," she demands, pushing herself onto me even harder.

I pinch her nipple with one hand, then her clit with the other, squeezing them both as I pull out slowly, then ram myself back into her.

Her slick walls squeeze me like a vice, and I build up a faster, punishing pace. I'm so close now. I can feel my balls tighten, there's no way in hell I'll let go before she does.

"I need you to come for me, baby. Come right fucking now." I ram into her, my balls slapping against her pussy. At my command, her core quakes around my cock as she cries out in pleasure. Finally, I let go, my balls emptying everything I have into her sweet heat.

Hayden

I wake the next morning with a delicious soreness between my legs that puts a smile on my face. We had made love at least four more times last night. Finally, near dawn, exhaustion took over.

I hear movement in the kitchen and smile again. Wrench. He's most likely making breakfast. That's one thing he has spoiled me with. Breakfast and coffee I don't have to fix myself.

The few times that I have cooked for him, he had blown my mind, doing the dishes himself. He hadn't allowed me to help at all. My ex used to give me absolute hell if I didn't clean up immediately after he finished eating.

I'm convinced Wrench is a damn unicorn—rare and magical. The thought makes me giggle, just as I'm stepping into the kitchen.

"What's so funny?" Wrench from the stove wearing the apron Hanley had given me for Mother's day. The saying across the front nearly does me in. "Sprinkled with Fairy Dust."

"Nice apron." I giggle again.

Wrench smirks. "I think I look quite dashing in it." He bats his eyelashes rapidly, and neither of us can hold back our laughter.

"You're such a weirdo," I inform him, shaking of my head.

"But, I'm your weirdo."

My heart pounds quickly in my chest. "Guess that makes me yours?"

"Damn straight you're mine." He moves to me, wrapping his arms around my waist, his lips claiming mine in a deep, panty-melting kiss.

Just then, the front door to my house slams against the inside wall. "Hayden!"

"In the kitchen," I call, giving Wrench an apologetic smile.

That smile fades when Austin appears in my kitchen, a wild-eyed look on his face, and his chest heaving like he had run all the way here.

"Austin? What's wrong?"

"She's missing." He swallows hard.

My heart sinks in my chest. "Who? Who is missing?"

"Hanley! Mom went in to wake her for church, but she wasn't there. At first we thought maybe she just went outside to play, but her little purse was still there, on the bed. You know she never goes anywhere without it. And the window..." His entire body sags against the doorframe.

"What about the window?" I can't breathe.

"The latch was broken from the outside. It looked like someone shoved something up in there to break it. They left the window open when they left. I'm so sorry, Hayden. I'm so fucking sorry." Austin's voice breaks.

I'm watching his lips move and hearing his words, desperately trying to understand, but around me the world is spinning faster and faster, making my knees wobble beneath me.

Wrench's arms are back around me, literally holding me up. "It's okay, baby. We'll find her."

I turn and bury my face in his neck. "But how? We don't even know who took her."

"Maybe. But do you remember that watch I gave her last week? I told her to never take it off, not even during bath time because it was waterproof?"

I nod and Austin pushes away from the wall, the despair on his face fading, just a little.

"It's a tracking device. I can find her, but I'll need to go to the clubhouse. Snake has the whole thing set up on his computer."

Him giving my daughter a tracking device is something we will need to discuss later, but right now, we need to find Hanley.

"I need to get dressed," I whisper, turning to head toward the bedroom. My phone rings as I get there. Eric's name is on the phone screen.

"Eric?"

"Thank fuck you answered. I just got back to my office. There was a message left for me from a parole officer. Apparently, they released Henry into a halfway house. He's supposed to stay there and follow the rules for a year before being completely released into the world. He didn't even make it a week, though. The motherfucker is missing."

"Oh shit, Eric," I sob, sinking down onto the bed, the phone clutched tightly in my hand.

"Hayden? What's wrong?" Suddenly, Wrench is there, plucking the phone from my fingers as I stare blankly in front of me.

He has my baby.

"Eric, this is Wrench." Silence pounds in my eardrums as Wrench listens to Eric speak. "Fuck, man. Hanley is missing too. Someone snatched her from her bed in the middle of the night."

There's another pause as he listens.

"Yeah, brother. Let us know when you land. We'll have a car waiting for you." Wrench hangs up and kneels before me.

"He took her, didn't he?" I whisper.

Wrench nods. "I think so, baby. But you can't fall apart yet. I need you. I need you to help us find her. Where he would take her? Does he know anyone in this area?"

"I don't know." My body trembles.

"It's okay, baby. We're gonna find her. I promise you."

Chapter 7
Wrench

Mina and the girls are waiting for us as we get to the clubhouse. They surround Hayden, offering the support she needs so much.

Once I know she's being taken care of, I head for the room where we hold our church meetings. Every member of the club is already there, taking up every single chair and lining the walls of the room.

Timber had filled everyone in on the facts, including the part about Henry going missing from the halfway house.

"Why the fuck did no one notify her that his ass was being released? That's what I want to know," Bear growls from across the room. "You'd think the victim would be told when their abuser is running free."

"We don't know for sure that Henry is the one that has her," Gear interjects.

His twin, Sprocket, shakes his head. "You don't seriously think that's a coincidence, do you?"

Gear sighs, frustrated. "No, not really. But I can hope she's just playing somewhere, and not being held by her abusive father, who should have been offed in prison."

"Snake, have you found anything yet?" Timber asks.

Snake shakes his head. "I've been checking all the feeds from every camera I can, but this would go a lot faster if I knew what he was driving. It's a safe bet he paid with cash. That also brings up the question: where the hell did he get the money and the car to drive all the way here from West fucking Virginia?"

My blood turns to ice in my veins. *Where did that fucker take her?*

"Right now, I'm trying to remotely turn on her watch tracker. It's not picking up for some reason. That is only possible if she's in an area with a lot of tree cover getting between the watch and a satellite."

Timber looks over at me. "His brother, Eric? You trust him? Would he help him do this?"

I shake my head. "I honestly don't think so, Prez. He seemed pretty genuine about his feelings for Hanley and Hayden. Besides, he's on his way here now. He was already on a private jet, headed this way when he called Hayden to let her know Henry was missing."

"When is his plane supposed to land?"

"In about four more hours. I said we'd send a car to pick him up."

"Goose, you and Ringo, be there to pick him up. Snake, keep trying to find something. If you get that tracker turned on, let me know immediately. The rest of you, stay on the compound and keep your eyes open. As soon as

Snake can pinpoint her location, we are heading out." Once Timber finishes handing out his orders, everyone stands and heads out the door.

I stay seated at the table, lost in thought. What if Henry did take her? What if he plans on hurting that little girl to get back at her mother for sending him to jail? What if we can't find her in time?

I'm pulled from my thoughts by Timber as he takes a seat next to me.

"We'll get her back. You know we will. And if that mother fucker survives it, he can go right back to prison."

I grit my teeth. "I have no plans for that fucker to remain on the same planet as my girls."

"That may be hard to accomplish with his brother here, don't you think?"

I meet his hard gaze. "Something tells me Eric would stay quiet."

"You need to know for sure before it happens. I don't think those two girls of yours would like visiting you behind glass for the rest of your life." Timber slaps my shoulder as he stands, then exits out of the room, leaving me alone with that thought.

Eric will keep his mouth shut or I'll bury his ass with his brother. I don't give a fuck. All I care about right now is finding my sweet Hanley and bringing her home safely. I swore I would protect her. She had paid me to be her bodyguard,   after   all.

Hayden

I don't know what I'd do if it weren't for Mina and the girls. They've stayed close to me since we got here, thinking nothing of it when I break down into tears. They just take turns hugging me until I stop.

"Shouldn't we call the police or something?" I ask, after several hours of waiting.

"That would *not* be a good idea," Mina says slowly.

"Why not?"

"The club takes care of its own," Fiona informs me. "And sometimes means doing things that aren't exactly legal."

My eyes grow wide. *Aren't exactly legal? What the fuck have I gotten myself into?*

"You're scaring her, Fi," Bella warns from her place on the couch, where she's feeding her daughter.

"Let me try it another way," Miranda says, her eyes focusing on mine. "If you could get your hands on whoever took your daughter, what would you do to them?"

"I'd kill them." And I would, too.

"If you had the chance to kill them, would you *really* do it, though?" The room falls silent, waiting for my answer.

I pause a moment, trying to imagine, but all I can think about is Hanley, kidnapped and afraid and crying out for me. "Fuck yes."

"Now you know exactly what I meant," Fiona says, sitting back with Justice, Bella's little boy, in her lap.

Just then, Wrench walks into the room and I jump up, running over to him. "Anything?"

"Not yet. Snake thinks they're somewhere with a lot of trees blocking the signal. We're hoping we'll get something soon, though." He presses his lips into my hair and whispers, "I'm so sorry this is happening."

Tears burn my eyes, and I blink to hold them back. "Neither of us could have predicted this. But I have to ask, what made you think to give her that watch?"

"It's actually a prototype that Snake was looking into for the club. We wanted something we could use for all you girls—and the kids—to help keep everyone safe. If anything happened, we'd be able to locate you quickly."

"Hanley seemed so scared, and I just had this weird feeling. I wanted to be sure I could always find her. The watch even has a panic button on the side, but I never had time to show it to her. Now I wish I had."

"Let's hope it actually works." I choke back tears and bury myself in his chest, breathing him in. I love this man so much, and when all of this is over, I need to make sure he knows it.

"Eric should be here any time," he assures me. "Maybe he knows something we haven't thought of yet."

God, please, help me find my baby girl.

Wrench

We're almost finished bringing Eric up to speed when Snake comes running into the room with his laptop in his hands. "I've got something."

He takes a seat at the table and we all crowd in behind him.

"You turn on the signal?" Timber asks.

"Actually, no. The panic button was triggered. I don't know how, but thank fuck it was. It turns on the built-in microphone, so that we can hear what's going on."

"Where the fuck did you get this thing?" I ask.

"That's classified," Snake murmurs as he turns up the volume. What I hear makes my heart break.

"Pease let me out. I be good." Hanley is crying, a pounding sound nearly drowning out the sound of her sobs.

"Stop beating on that door before I give you something to cry about, you little shit! Your mother should have aborted you. She thinks she can leave me for that biker? Ha! I don't fucking think so. I'll kill you both first."

We have to strain to hear that last part. His voice grows quieter, as if he's walking away.

Hanley's sobs are quiet now, as if she's afraid to make any sounds at all. Snake turns the volume down.

Trying to hold in my anger, I breathe through my nose, but it's no use. My neck feels hot and clammy.

"The signal is coming from the mountains. About thirty miles from here. From the sounds we heard, they have to be in a cabin or building."

He taps away furiously at the keyboard. "So I set the coordinates to get a satellite view of the area. This is it."

A satellite view of a tiny building nestled in the trees appears on his screen.

"Doesn't look like a very big cabin," Bear says.

"It's most likely an old abandoned hunting shack." Timber looks closer at the screen. "I've hunted there before. Zoom out. There should be another cabin about a mile south." Once it's on the screen, he shakes his head and taps one area to the bottom. "We'll go in from there. He won't even notice we're there 'til it's too late."

"I'm coming too," Eric says. I had almost forgotten he was here. Timber gives me a look I know too well before he ushering the others out of the room.

"I don't know if that is a good idea."

"Look, I'm not stupid. I know there's a reason you haven't involved the police. I suspect that Henry is about to disappear. Never to be heard from again."

I hold his gaze, my face hard. "The question is, are you okay with that?"

"My father and I are both more than okay with that."

I frown. "Your father knows about this too?"

"He doesn't know all the details, but let's just say, I was sent here to make sure that Henry is never heard from again." His admission takes me by surprise.

"Won't your stepmom notice her son is just gone forever?"

Eric lifts a brow. "Seeing as he killed her, I would say probably not."

Ice shoots through my veins. "Hayden never mentioned that she'd died."

"She doesn't know yet. My father found her body an hour after learning Henry was missing. The cops suspect Henry, and so do we. He blamed her for not being on his side during the trial. She couldn't stand to even look at him and refused to be there."

I'm at a loss for words. How could that son of a bitch just kill his mother like that? "Fuck man, I'm sorry. It sounds like you were close to her."

"Yes, I was. She was the only mother I ever had, even though she came into my life when I was a teenager. She was always there for me. This time I will be there for her, to make sure her killer pays for what he's done."

"I guess we're on the same page then," I murmur.

"I guess we are."

Henry

That little bitch, and her bitch mother, thought they can hide from me? I never even wanted a kid, but my mother said I had to marry the whore. Fuck, I don't even believe the little bitch is mine. Why won't she shut up?

"STOP YOUR FUCKING CRYING!"

I can't even think with all this noise. I'm going outside. Maybe I can figure out my next move if I can't hear her.

"Daddy?"

"I'm not your daddy, you little bitch! I saw the way your whore of a mother was looking at the neighbors," I yell before slamming the door behind me.

Every time—every fucking time—I took her out to dinner, that whore was smiling at the servers.

Then she had that fucking prick, Austin, over at the house all the time. They were always whispering and giving each other googly eyes when they thought I wasn't looking. I'll teach that bitch how to give googly eyes, right after I rip them out of her fucking skull.

"I need diapers for the baby, the baby needs clothes, we gotta buy groceries." That fucking bitch was always nagging me for something. She never shut the fuck up. I'll shut her up, though. I'll shove my cock down her throat. Yes, that's

what I'll do. I'll shove my cock down her throat and shut her up forever.

I've got the kid now, so I know she'll do whatever I say, but I don't have her cell phone number. I Google her shop number, but nobody answers.

Fuck.

I know my prick of a brother knows how to reach her, though, so I pull up his number and fire him a text.

Me: Bro, give me the bitch's phone number

Eric: I don't have it

Me: Yes you do. I know you fucking talk to her. Give it to me

Eric: I don't have it

Throwing my phone across the clearing, I stalk back inside the cabin. I'm going to get that number one way or another and I bet the little bitch in the closet knows it.

"Oh Hanley, Daddy needs your help." I say as I open the closet door. She looks up at me with her big doe eyes. "I need your momma's phone number."

"Will…will you hurt Mommy?" she stutters.

"No, I only want to tell her where you are."

"But I don't know it, Daddy. It's in my purse."

"Well, where is your purse?"

"It's in my room at Austin's Mama's house."

"Fuck!" I scream, glaring at her terrified face and then slamming the door closed once again.

Think, Henry. Think.

Once the little bitch is finally quiet, I grab a chair and get comfortable. I need to think.

"Daddy, I'm hungry." Her small voice sounds muffled from inside the closet.

"Shut the fuck up!" I roar.

I go back outside to get away from her nagging. Just like her fucking bitch mother. Nag, nag, nag.

My phone right rings from the tall grass to my left, right where I'd hurled it. On the screen is a missed call from a number I don't recognize. I decide to text Eric again.

Me: Bro, come on. Give me the whore's number. I only want to talk to her.

Me: Eric, you stinking little shithead, give me her number. I am your only brother. You're supposed to help me.

Me: If you don't give me her fucking number, I will show up where you live

Chapter 8
Wrench

It's nearly dark when we pull up to the old hunting cabin just south of where Henry is holding Hanley. We unload everything and are just strapping up when Eric's phone vibrates with text after text.

He pulls it out of his pocket to read them and his face goes dark.

"The stupid ass is texting me, asking for Hayden's phone number. As if I would actually give it to him." I stand behind him, looking over his shoulder, reading the texts as they come in.

"Don't give him shit," I warn. "I don't want Hayden getting a damn thing that would make her worry any more than she already is."

I watch as Eric answers Henry, acting as if he doesn't have it. Henry even has the balls to threaten Eric.

"Let's get moving," Timber says. "It's still another mile from here to the spot he's holed up in. I want to get there right at dark. Fucker won't see us coming."

Like soldiers, we line up, heading north toward my sweet girl.

I'm on my way, baby girl.

About an hour later, the little shack appears, standing in a small clearing. And sitting right there on the tiny porch, just outside of the door, is the fucker I want to see six feet under.

Timber uses hand signals to send Bear and Torque around to the right. He sends Gear and Sprocket around to the left. Hopefully, they can come at him from behind, getting the jump on Henry before he barricades himself inside. He could hurt Hanley if this doesn't go as planned. My heart rate kicks up. I need to get to her before he can.

Henry is sitting closer to the side that Bear and Torque are coming from and we all watch quietly, holding our breath, as Torque presses himself along the side of the shack and silently draws closer.

My lungs feel frozen in my chest as I watch for any indication that Henry notices us. We don't want to shoot yet. Not until Hanley is safe.

A twig snaps beneath Torque's foot and Henry jumps to attention. Torque doesn't give him time to react further. Instead, he jumps around the corner, slamming the steel pipe in his hands down on Henry's head. The fucker drops immediately.

"Fuck," Blood grumbles. "Did you kill him already? That's not fair."

I kneel and check the fucker's pulse, but there's nothing there.

"I'd say he's dead. Thanks a lot, Torque," I huff.

"Well, I can't help the fucker has a soft head!" Torque throws his arms up in the air, exasperated, and everyone laughs.

"Move. I gotta go find my girl." I shake my head, annoyed as I walk inside.

Looking around, I only see one door. That has to be a closet. I don't hear any sounds as I approach. It's locked from the outside. Sliding the lock open, I gently open the door, praying Hanley is okay.

She's there, lying on the floor, sound asleep. Kneeling down, I push her silky hair away from her face. As I do so, her eyes flutter open and an enormous smile spreads across her face.

"My favortist bodyguard," she whispers, as I pull her up into a hug.

"You okay, sweetie? Are you hurt anywhere?" I hold her away from me, trying to get a good look at her.

"I okay now. I just want mommy." Her little lip wobbles as if she is going to cry.

"And your mommy can't wait to see you." I pick her up, cradling her face in my neck as we walk back outside. I don't want her to see anything if the guys haven't moved Henry's body yet.

"Cleanup has been taken care of," Timber says. "Let's get her back to the clubhouse. The doc can look her over there."

I hold Hanley closer to me as we head back to the vehicles, and notice Blood disappearing into the trees and instantly feel satisfied. If anyone knows how to make a dead body disappear forever, it's Blood.

Hayden

When they pull into the drive, I run out, sobbing, jerking open the passenger side door. Hanley jumps out into my arms in an instant and I hold her as tight as I can, so thankful to have my baby back.

"Are you okay? Did he hurt you?" I look her over from her head to her feet.

"I okay, mommy. My bodyguard came to get me. Daddy left me in a closet. I'm hungry. Can we go eat now? Wrench said we can eat whatever I want," she says.

"Yes, baby, we'll go eat, but I want the doctor to look at you first."

Luckily for her, that process doesn't take long, because an hour later, we are sitting at a table, watching Hanley eat a pizza. The doctor found nothing wrong with her physically, thank God, but suggested we get her in to see a therapist as soon as possible.

Wrench and I have already noticed that she won't let either of us out of her sight. And for now, I don't want her out of my sight either.

So many things could have happened. Both Hanley and I would probably be dead by now if we hadn't had the help of the club. Their methods may be illegal, but they sure know how to take care of their own.

"Hanley said that Henry is gone. Was he not at the cabin when you guys got there?" I whisper to Wrench, keeping my voice low so she doesn't hear.

"He was there. She just didn't see him." Wrench doesn't explain further.

"Where is he? Did someone take him into the police station?" I ask in confusion.

"No." He stares at me a beat and then sighs and leans in closer. "He's gone. He won't ever be coming back. That is all I can tell you. That's how this club works." He looks at me, his eyes pleading.

I sit quietly, realizing then that I really don't care how he's gone. I'm just happy that he is. And he deserves whatever happened to him.

"I love you, ya know?" I whisper, looking up into Wrench's eyes and smiling.

He reaches over, pushing my hair behind my ear. "I love you, too."

Chapter 9
Wrench

Since we had rescued Hanley from that awful closet, she hasn't let me or her mom out of her sight. I've basically moved in since then, and things are getting better for her. Slowly.

She hasn't spent another night with Austin's mom, though, and she refuses to go over for a visit inside the house. The therapist said that it could take some time for her to get past everything that happened. So, we don't push her into anything she doesn't want to do.

Hayden had finally talked me into calling my mom and inviting her out for a visit. At first, our conversation on the phone felt a little uncomfortable. I did tell her that I had found "the one", and asked if she would come out and meet her.

Mom had seemed more excited about having a grandchild then she was about actually hearing from me. I can't really blame her, though. I'd treated her horribly. Hopefully, I can get her to forgive me once she gets here.

"Who's picking your mom up from the airport?" Hayden asks as she walks into the kitchen.

"Miranda," I say. "Fiona and Mina are busy getting ready for the Poison Pen's opening tomorrow. We'll meet them at the clubhouse around five this evening."

"You're not going to give her boyfriend a hard time, are you?" Hayden grins when I give her a look of mock innocence.

"I've no idea what you mean. Besides, what if he's a sensitive pencil pusher? We don't need that type in this family."

"She didn't tell you anything about him?"

"Nope. She said it was a surprise. Wouldn't even tell me his name because she was afraid I'd have Snake look into his background."

Hayden laughs. "He's probably nothing like you expect."

Its five o'clock and we're at the clubhouse, waiting for my mom to get here. Miranda had texted to say she had picked them up, but refused to give me any details about the guy my mom is with. Apparently, my mom threatened death. I can't help but to roll my eyes at that. Although I do believe my mom is capable of that, I highly doubt she'd give a warning beforehand.

Miranda walks in. My mom trails inside behind her, and I rush over, pulling her into a bear hug. I hadn't realized how much I had missed her, until now. I don't cry, but even now, tears of happiness prick at my eyes.

"I've missed you," I whisper into her hair, before pulling back to get a good look at her.

"I've missed you too, sweet boy." She smiles. "I want you to meet someone. This is Chucky."

She steps away, and I finally get a good look at the guy standing behind her. He's definitely nothing like I expected. And he's wearing a cut that announces him to be a part of Night Howler's MC, North Mississippi chapter.

"Holy shit," I say. "You're from Reaper's MC. His sister Mina is our President's ole lady."

"Yeah, I was actually out of town when they went to New Orleans to help. When I told Reaper where we were headed, he sent a package for me to deliver to Timber."

"Chucky?" Mina comes rushing into the room. "What are you doing here?"

"It's a long story, but let me introduce to you the one and only, Maria. She also happens to be Wrench's mom." He smiles down at my mom.

"So this is the woman that's had you so heart-broken all those years? It's so good to meet you!" Mina wraps my mom up in a hug.

My mom grins and then stands up tall and looks around the room. "Now, where's my grandbaby?"

Hayden and I laugh, and we lead her to the kitchen. Inside, Hanley is sneaking cookies. And that is when I think my mother falls completely in love with her.

Later that evening, I'm sitting alone with my mom by the firepit.

"Mom, I need to apologize to you."

She frowns. "Apologize for what?"

"For how I've treated you the last few years. You didn't deserve it."

My mom pats my hand. "Zack, there really isn't anything to forgive. You're my son. I love you. I always will. I know you've been pissed off at the world. Most young people are. Then they tend to take it out on those they love. I forgave you two seconds later, every single time." She shrugs her shoulders like it's no big deal.

My chest grows tight as I think of how I've hurt her. "I still want to say I am sorry. You've always been there for me, and I've treated you like shit. I love you mom."

She leans over, pulling me into a hug.

"I love you too, sweet boy." I roll my eyes at her use of the word "boy". "Now, I expect more grandbabies, and don't forget to marry that girl somewhere in there. Hopefully soon."

I blink up at her, serious all of the sudden. "What if she says no?"

Mom raises an eyebrow. "What if she says yes?"

Little does she know, I want to ask her. But I need Hayden to say yes. I can't live without her. She is my salvation.

Hayden

Wrench's mom stayed for a week before they had to head back to Mississippi. We promised to visit them as soon as we were able.

I'm working at my office today, while Wrench is at the shop with the guys. Hanley had wanted to stay with him, so I'm quite sure she's covered in grease by now. I'm hoping her fascination with motors is just a phase.

I have no problems with a girl who wants to be a mechanic, but I'd like for her to love dresses and frilly things just a little longer.

"HayHay, there's a man here to see you. He said it was a legal matter and wouldn't tell me anything else," Austin interrupts my thoughts from the door.

"A legal matter? Send him back." I frown, unsure what legal matter anybody could possibly have to discuss with me. Am I being sued for something?

A man in a suit walks through my door. He's an older gentleman and definitely looks like the lawyer type.

"Mrs. Lynn? I'm Gary Brown, attorney for the late Mr. Barron and Sandra LaRue, your grandparents." He offers his hand, which I ignore as I stand there speechless.

"Don't call them my grandparents. They lost that title the day they refused to take me in. Why are you here?" I try not to take my anger out on him. He's just doing whatever job he was sent to do.

"Yes, well, I am here because it was never Mr. Barron's intention to not take you or provide for you. He died of a heart attack two days before you were born, but months before that, he named his daughter, your mother and her offspring, as the sole beneficiaries of most of his estate." He hands me a stack of papers.

I gape over at him. "What? How is this possible? Wouldn't I have known about this before now?"

"It's kind of a long story. I have not always been the attorney for this estate. It was actually the job of my father's business partner. When he passed away, it landed on my desk. By the time I was able to go through all the files, Mrs. LaRue had also passed."

"For years, she told everyone that her daughter had died, but never mentioned a child being born. I was originally looking for the closest living relative to inherit the estate, when I came across your birth record. From there, I was able to track you through your foster care records, until I found you here, in Montana."

I gape at him in shock, unable to really comprehend what is on the papers in front of me.

"So what you're telling me is…"

"You are inheriting roughly three million dollars. It's not all cash, of course. There are stocks, bonds, a couple houses in various places, as well as a ranch. It's kind of funny to find you in Montana, because the ranch you now own isn't very far from here." He shuffles papers around on my desk until he finds the one he's looking for and points.

There, on the paper, is an old horse ranch that looks to be just on the other side of the Wolf's Ridge property. Right where the MC has cabin rentals.

"Holy shit," I whisper, plopping down into my chair.

"I can tell you're a bit overwhelmed," Mr. Brown continues. "I'll be staying in town for a few days to go over everything with you, and get you to sign all the necessary documents transferring ownership over to you. Would you like to set a time to meet with me tomorrow? That gives you a chance to read through all the documents."

I nod. "I can meet you here at nine? Could I go out to the ranch and have a look around?"

"That will be fine. I have the keys to everything back at my hotel. I will see you in the morning." He bids me farewell and leaves my office while I gape down at the papers in front of me.

Chapter 10
Wrench

"I can't believe you own all of this," I say, looking around at the orchard sitting at one side of the property.

"I still can't believe it myself."

I sigh, taking in the beauty of the mountainside. "Have you decided what you want to do with it? I mean, you could fix the old barns and the fences. Make it into a working horse ranch again."

I look over at my beautiful girl, who is smiling with her eyes closed. She's so beautiful in this setting. The ring in my pocket reminds me of a very important question I still need to ask.

"I was talking to the girls about it last week, and Mina said something that sparked an idea." Her gaze meets mine, her face filled with an expression I can't quite read.

"You want to share this idea?"

"Wolf's Ridge is just through those trees. We could easily make a road between the two, get horses in here, and offer dude ranch type packages to the clientele. It would bring in even more business to the MC every year. Many people from the bigger cities are drawn to places like that. Makes them feel like they're living the rustic life, even if just for a little while."

I consider that. "That's actually not a bad idea."

"You think Timber and the others would go for it? Because we would essentially be in business together, and we aren't actually together, together. You know?" She watches me, her lip tucked under her teeth as if afraid of what I will say.

I can't help but smile as I reach into my pocket and pull out the ring.

"I want us to be together, together. You know?" I hold my breath, still afraid she might say no. "Will you marry me?"

"You really want to marry me?" Tears glisten in her eyes.

I pull her close and gaze down into her smiling face. "I absolutely really want to marry you."

"Yes," she breathes out, just before my mouth takes hers.

Hayden

I watch the sun dance off the engagement ring on my hand, and still can't believe I'm engaged.

"It's a beautiful ring." Mina smiles at me, catching me looking at it again.

"It's perfect," I sigh.

"When will construction begin on the new barns and paddocks?" Miranda asks from her chair next to the picnic table.

The MC has a cook out every Saturday to bring everyone together as a family. I have learned that is exactly what the MC is. Family. It doesn't matter where you come from, or who your blood family is, the MC family is a lot thicker than blood.

"The contractor said they'll get started next week. As long as the schedule stays on track, we should be ready to open by the spring."

"We should start advertising now. Try to fill up the calendar for next year. I suspect it'll get so full, people will need to make reservations a year in advance," Bella says, looking up from the book she is reading.

"Is that Mina's newest release?" I ask, nodding toward it.

"Yep, and let me just say that since she and Timber have gotten together, her sex scenes have gone off the charts." She keeps her eyes on the book in her hands, turning the page, as if afraid to miss a single word.

Mina's cheeks turn pink with embarrassment. "Geez, girl. Point out how innocent I was, why don't ya?"

That gets a laugh out of all of us.

"When are you and Wrench going to set a date?" Miranda asks.

"I'm not sure," I admit. "We haven't really talked about it."

Mina sits up, suddenly excited. "Why don't we all do it at the same time?"

I lift my brows in surprise. "Me, you and Miranda?"

She nods. "Yeah. All three at once, get it over with. We can do it here. Have a huge after-party and everything."

"Sounds good to me. But when?"

"Before Mina pops would be a good idea," Bella murmurs, and we all laugh again.

"Let's do it next week, because we have the opening of Poison Pen coming up, and honestly, I don't know if I can hold this little one in that long." Mina sighs, rubbing her stomach.

"Next week it is," I say. "Now, who volunteers to tell the guys?"

"Tell us what?" Timber's voice comes from behind us and I look back to find the three men we were just talking about, waiting for us to answer.

"We're all getting married next week," Mina informs him. "All three couples. It's not up for discussion or debate. It's happening before our baby pops out."

Mina stares them down, as if daring them to say otherwise, but the guy's just chuckle.

"And what, may I ask, is so funny?" Miranda crosses her arms over her chest like she's ready to do battle.

"We were just coming to let you ladies know that everything is already set up, and we will be getting married next week. It's not up for debate." All three smile at us as if they won the lottery.

"Oh," Miranda, Mina and I say at the same time.

After a few more silent moments, everyone bursts into laughter.

Chapter 11
One Year Later
Wrench

Wolf's Landing opened to guests a little more than a month ago. The girls went crazy last year, running ads all over the country, and it didn't take long for reservations to pour in. We already have a waiting list.

"Daddy!" Hanley calls, running toward the barn, where me and the guys are unloading a load of hay. The sound of her calling me Daddy still causes such pride when I hear it.

"I'm right here, kiddo. What's wrong?" I catch her as she launches herself into my arms.

"Nothing." She grins sweetly, and I can tell by that alone that she's done something she wasn't supposed to.

"Are you sure? Because I see mommy headed this way and she doesn't look too happy." I look at my daughter waiting for her to tell me what she did,

"I didn't do anything, Daddy, but I have to go now. I be back later." She kisses my cheek as I set her down, then she takes off down toward the orchard.

Hayden comes along then, clearly out of breath, and I try not to smile at her predicament. Especially since I'm the one that helped get her that way.

"You are so sexy right now," I whisper, trying to hug her to me.

"Don't you try to distract me, Wrench. I am hugely pregnant. My feet hurt, and I am tired. There are guests ready to have breakfast, and I don't have any eggs, because Hanley decided there were baby chickens inside them. I have no idea where she hid them!"

I try my best to keep a straight face as she explains the situation. I almost succeed too, until Timber opens his big mouth.

"Well, we do have a rooster in there." Timber's words send every man in the barn into fits of laughter.

"I blame all of you," Hayden grumbles. "Now go find those eggs!" Hayden stomps her foot, turns around and leaves the barn without so much as a goodbye.

"Looks like we're Easter egg hunting boys."

Everyone groans.

"You shouldn't have told her where baby chickens come from," I say to Timber as we walk out of the barn.

"Better than her thinking they come from a fucking stork."

"Good thing she hasn't asked how the new baby got inside her mom. You'd probably tell it all." I say as I look under a bush.

"Hell no. Far as any of our little girls will ever know, babies just appear when you're in love, and boys have a disease that will get on you if you stand too close to them."

I laugh. "What are you going to do when Luna is old enough to date?"

Their daughter, Luna, was born only ten months after their son, Hawk. He's been a nervous wreck ever since. The guys are always giving us hell about all the things girls can get up to. Especially Blood, whose only child, Hunter, is a year old. When Blood and Miranda have a girl, I can't wait to give him the same kind of nightmares he's given us.

"I need to buy more fucking ammo," Timber says, grabbing his phone, probably to call his wife as I laugh at his retreating back.

Although now that I think about it, I probably should get on that as well. No way in hell will anyone be good enough for my sweet Hanley.

The End, For Now.

About The Author

Marissa Ann spends her time in rural North Mississippi with her husband, the kids and all of their animals on a hobby farm.

She always said she would write books one day even though many thought she never would. She made a promise to a childhood friend who left this world for the next in 2015. That she would finally write and publish at least one.

Her first book hit the market in 2018 and she's never looked back. She now has several out with many more scheduled for release. Want to stay up to date with new releases, giveaways and all the cool things?

Website:
www.authormarissaann.com
Facebook:
https://www.facebook.com/MarissaAnnAuthor
Instagram:
https://www.instagram.com/authormarissaann/
Twitter:
https://twitter.com/marissaannbooks
Goodreads:
https://www.goodreads.com/author/show/18159855.Marissa_Ann
Linkedin:
https://www.linkedin.com/in/marissa-ann-ballard-93982b186/
Tik Tok
https://www.tiktok.com/@authormarissaann

Wolfsbane Ridge MC Book 4, Bear's Savior

Sara: sharp, responsible, determined
Bear: mature, powerful, repentant

While taking time away from her studies to be a
nurse to help her family's business, Sara Blackcat
meets and falls for an older man. She and Bear
spend one glorious night together, but Bear
regrets it thinking he's too old for the younger
woman. She's determined to show him love
knows no number.

With only a few days left until graduation and
completing her dream of becoming a registered
nurse, Sara is working a clinical shift at the local
hospital when a man comes in brandishing a
firearm. Sara manages to send a text before the
gunman confiscates all the phones.

When the Wolfsbane Ridge MC finds out what is
going on, they jump to action. The people and
town are theirs to protect. Bear becomes fiercely
protective when he finds out Sara is in the
hospital in the hands of this madman.

Will he reach her in time to save her?
Will he realize how he really feels about her, that
        love knows no age? COMING SOON!!

**Sneak Peak of Poison Pen Series, Book 2,
Lily's Shadow
Prologue
LilyAnna**

It has been almost six months since I moved to White Summer. My best friend Fiona opened her tattoo shop in town and hired me as her office manager-artist. One of her requirements for me to work for her has been to attend self defense classes.

I was doing really well in my class in Seattle, even taking extra classes because I love it so much. Fiona has promised to teach me kickboxing; she is really good at it. Sometimes she even wins against her own trainer, Austin.

After Fiona's boyfriend was kidnapped by a stalker recently, I asked her to increase my training. I even want to learn how to use a gun. It was my fault. I'm the one that left her keys on the counter.

No matter how many times she tells me it wasn't. I can't help but feel guilty about it. I don't ever want to see one of my friend's look so helpless again. Good thing Fiona is a kick ass bitch and took down the monster all on her own.

Fiona and Baratta are leaving for vacation to Italy after Miranda has her baby, so I need to up my game. I will be running the tattoo shop on my own for the first time. She's depending on me to keep everything running smoothly while they are gone.

I have my first martial arts class with Austin today. I'm really excited about it but I'm nervous as hell too. Austin is an attractive man. Every time I look at him my heart starts racing. I doubt he even realizes I exist beyond being a client of Hay's Den.

I'm about to grab my gym bag to head out of the door when Loki, my German shepherd starts to whine. Looking over at him, I see that he has his food bowl hanging from his mouth.

"I'm sorry, did I forget to fill it this morning?" I laugh as he hops around excitedly as I take the bowl from him.

Filling the bowl, I place it on the floor. He licks my face as I stroke his fur.

"My sweet boy." I murmur into his head.

I got him several years ago from a trainer I met while at the inker's expo. He trained guard dogs for the elite and gave me a hell of a deal for him. He's been my constant companion ever since. One thing is for sure, he'd eat someone's face off if I told him to. That comes in handy for a single woman these days. Smiling at the thought, I pick up my gym bag and walk out the door.

Austin

Moving to White Summer a little over a year ago has been the best decision I have ever made. I am working at Hay's den, my boss is my best friend and life is more laid back here. Something I've needed for quite some time.

I'm no longer fighting professionally although I miss it sometimes. The roar of the fans, the adrenaline rush of winning, the women throwing their bras and panties in the ring after a match.

I don't miss the circus created by my ex wife though. I found out she was sleeping with one of my sponsors and kicked her out. In retaliation she accused me of domestic violence.

After that I hired a private investigator. I discovered more than I ever expected. For example the reason the paparazzi always seemed to know where we were is because she called them.

About 2 months after the separation, I found out she was pregnant too. When confronted she said the baby wasn't mine. At that point I just wanted her out of my life so I didn't fight anything she wanted in the divorce.

After that, it didn't take Hayden long to convince me to move here with her. She was going through her own shit around that time as well. I probably would have killed her ex-husband if the police hadn't found him first.

My ex has started up her shit again lately. I had messages on my phone from her again last night. I didn't even bother checking them. Wish the bitch would get a fucking clue. I'm no longer interested.

I'm in the gym pounding the shit out of a bag when Lily comes in for her first advanced class with me. She has been in the beginner's class with Hayden, but after some shit down at the tattoo parlor she works in she really kicked it up a notch and we feel she's ready.

We just finished class, I tell her to head to the shower when a commotion breaks out at the front desk. I can hear Hayden yelling all the way back here so I know it's not good.

Lily and I approach cautiously. We can see a crowd gathered behind the desk. Hayden is facing us, yelling at a woman that has her back to us. The woman seems familiar but I can't see her face yet.

"Get out of my building!" Hayden yells.

"I am not leaving until I see him." The woman yells back. I know that voice; it's one I never wanted to hear again.

"If you don't leave on your own, I will have you escorted out!"

"Fine, you tell him if he ever wants to see his kid, I'm staying out at the Wolfsbane ridge cabins."

"Not for long." I hear one of the guys in the crowd murmur, just before she turns around and sees me.

"What do you want Erica?"

Instead of the defiant woman arguing with Hay Hay, she suddenly turns into a simpering damsel.

"I want you to come home, our daughter needs you."

"You said the baby wasn't mine, and this is my home."

"I lied, please give us another chance."

If I am sure of one thing, it is that I don't want her back. She ruined my career, my reputation and my life. I feel the eyes of everyone looking at me, so I do the first thing I can think of.

Throwing my arm around Lily, "Erica, meet my fiancée Lily." I'm hoping like hell Lily will go along with it.

I can feel her stiffening up before she relaxes into me. Looking down, Lily smiles up at me before turning her eyes to Erica.

"What about our daughter?" Erica whines.

"I'll contact our attorney first thing in the morning about getting a DNA test. But be warned Erica, if that baby belongs to Austin? We plan to go after sole custody. And we *will* win. My father happens to be Governor Mark Harris from California." Lily smirks at Erica's wide eyed expression. "Now get the fuck out!"

I hear the commotion as some of the Wolfsbane Ridge guys escort Erica out but I can't seem to take my eyes off of Lily. I'm shocked speechless at her admission to being the daughter of one of the most well known Governors.

I'm also shocked at my body's reaction to having her in my arms. I've tried very hard to keep it professional where she is concerned. If she remains in my arms though, all bets are off.

Chapter 1
Lily

Oh My God! I can't believe Austin just called me his fiancée! Then he put his arm around me. I must be dreaming. Who the fuck is this bitch? I watch out the front window as she pulls out her cell phone. I think she must be calling for a ride. When she puts the phone up to her ear, I notice one of the neighborhood strays that we sneak food out to, walk up and sniff her feet.

I don't even try to hold back my grin when he lifts his leg, but when he pisses on her fancy boots I lose control and start laughing hysterically. A few of the people in the room saw it happen and laughed with me but Austin must have missed it because he is giving me a strange look.

One of the motorcycle club members comments that he is going to feed that dog a steak. I'm not sure which one he is, I don't really associate with them often. They are Fiona's friends and family. Even though she is my bff, and I hold no bad feelings for them, I'm not about that lifestyle. I just want to do my job as a tattoo artist.

As soon as the laughter dies down the room starts to clear out. The drama seems to be over for now. I can see that Austin wants to say something but I put my hand over his mouth.

"Explanations can wait. I need a shower. Meet me back out here in twenty, and then I have an hour before the shop opens."

He quickly agrees and we part ways. When I get to the locker room I notice that I have it all to myself. I turn up the water to let it warm while I seek out towels and grab my gym bag. I have to hurry; I can already feel my muscles starting to tighten up from my class.

Standing under the hot stream, I lean my head back and close my eyes. Oh God, Austin Montgomery called me his fiancée. I just can't get over the thrill running through my body at those words. Thinking about him makes me feel needy. Grabbing my bar of soap, I run it down my sides, feeling the tight muscles of my abdomen but I don't stop there.

Working towards my aching pussy, I intentionally drop the soap. I slip my sudsy hands between my thighs. Immediately finding my clit, I rub myself gently at first.

I imagine Austin on his knees in front of me worshipping my body, his green eyes, searing into my soul. I pretend my fingers are his, strong yet flexible digits stroking my most sensitive spot. I start rubbing harder, feeling my release close in on me.

I'm almost there. The lights are flickering in the corner of my eyes. My moans are so loud they are echoing back to me from the shower walls. I'm about to implode when a sudden noise catches all my attention. Shit! Someone is knocking on the door. I quickly rinse and grab my things, running for the lockers to get dressed.

I don't even bother with trying to dry my hair. Shoving everything back into my bag I leave the locker room. When I step out the door to my utter horror, Austin is there leaning against the wall staring up at the ceiling. I take just a moment to admire his tall muscular frame, until I remember what he just interrupted.

"I ummm have to go." I blurt out

"I thought the shop didn't open for a bit. Can we talk, please?"

"Oh yeah sorry. Wanna walk with me?"

He looks down at his watch. "I don't have much time either but I can walk you to Poison Pen."

Austin

She said twenty minutes but when Lily didn't come out of the locker room for almost thirty-five minutes, I got worried. I open the door just a crack so I can call out to her but when I hear the unmistakable moans coming from the shower I quickly back out and knock on the door. I know she is the only one in there.

Only a few minutes go by when I hear her grab the door. I quickly lean against the wall and look up at the ceiling, acting like I don't know what she was doing in there.

Her face is red and she isn't making eye contact with me when she stutters out that she has to go. I realize her taking extra time in the shower means we don't have as much time to talk now, so I offer to walk her to work.

Once we get outside I just walk next to her. I'm not sure what it is about Lily but being near her relaxes me. She's not loud and outgoing like Fiona but she isn't a wilting flower either. In the short time I've known her I've come to respect her.

I see Poison Pen getting closer and realize we haven't talked at all, yet. "Can I meet you after you get off work and get something to eat?"

"You do realize we don't close until 2 in the morning right?"

"Yes."

"You also realize nothing is open that late, right?"

"Yes, you can come to my house. I can cook you dinner and explain today. I promise to keep my hands to myself."

She is reaching for the door when I blurt out, "Her name is Erica, she's my ex-wife and she is a bad person."

Lily puts her hand on my shoulder, I think she is going to respond but instead she turns, disappearing inside the tattoo shop. I start to walk away before I realize I have no idea what to make for dinner. I turn back and open the shop door.

"Hey Lily"

"Yes Austin?"

"Are you allergic to anything?"

She just gives me an odd look.

"Anything you don't like or can't eat?"

"Oh, umm no. I'm good with anything."

With that I head back to the gym for my last class of the day. I'm finishing up my cleaning when Hay Hay pops in. I look around for the little munchkin.

"Where's Hanley?"

"I sent her off with Wrench. We need to talk."

Sighing I run my hands over my head and drop down on a bench.

"First off, Lily? You never said you were dating anyone and you tell me everything. Everything Austin, why wouldn't you tell me that?"

"I'm not really dating her. I just didn't know what else to say to make Erica leave."

"Does Lily know about your history? Why would she play along like that?"

"I don't know, I'm meeting her after the shop closes. I promised to cook dinner and tell her everything."

"Oh my God! Austin, you're cooking for Lily? She must be really special; you don't even cook for me." Hayden pouts.

I can feel my face turning red. Cooking is my guilty little pleasure. I took it up after all the shit went down with Erica. I needed a hobby and my mom always says, "A man who can cook, is one you don't let off the hook."

It took a long time for Mom to understand that Hayden and I felt more like siblings than friends. I did bow down to her pressure once.

I kissed Hayden with everything I had, but it was like kissing a mirror. Stale and empty. I love her but there was no flame, no zing, and no connection. We would always be just friends.

Next thing I know Hayden has a big grin on her face. She starts chanting, "Austin and Lily sitting in a tree." I put my hand over her mouth to stop her. "It's not like that. She just happened to be there at the right or maybe wrong time."

"So, about Erica. What does she want?" Hayden asks.

"I don't know. She's been calling me nonstop for the last couple weeks. At first I was just ignoring her calls, but then I blocked her. She knows she is supposed to call my lawyer, not me."

"You need to find out if Cordelia is yours."

"What? Who?" I look at her with confusion.

"The baby, her name is Cordelia." She states.

"How do you know that? I didn't even know that."

"Oh Austin." She sits down next to me and leans her head on my shoulder. "I know you block out that part of the world but I still have friends back home. Her cousin Heather was in my class, we talk sometimes."

I glance outside and notice how late it's getting. "Hay Hay I have to get to the grocery store before it closes. I promise I will tell Lily everything. I know she is your friend too, I hate that she got pulled into this but my brain just went blank. I didn't know what to do or say."

"Austin, this is a small town. People talk, you're going to have to convince her to play along until Erica leaves town."

"I know." I tell her before I kiss her on the forehead.

The trip to the grocery store is blissfully uneventful. I got there about twenty minutes before closing so it was basically empty. I am loading my car, when my cell phone rings. I glance down at the screen planning to ignore it but when I see the name "Ellen Montgomery" I know better.

"Mom." I answer.

"Austin James."

Uh oh the middle name clues me in that I am in trouble. I don't even bother starting the car; just sit behind the wheel waiting.

"Well, I'm waiting." She says after a minute of silence.

"Waiting for what Mom?" I sigh, knowing what is coming.

"Waiting for my son to tell me about the woman he is engaged to, that he never introduced to his mother. Waiting to hear how that Bitch found you."

"I found out tonight that Hayden has been in contact with some of her old friends. One of them is Erica's cousin. I'm willing to bet they realized I wouldn't be far from her."

"That explains that but tell me about this fiancée I have never met." She demands.

"Lily is a friend. You've met Fiona right?" I ask.

"Yes."

"Lily works for her at the tattoo shop. I've been teaching her self defense. She was standing next to me when Erica caused a scene at Hay's Den. My mind went blank; I just wanted her to go away. I wasn't thinking, it just spilled out of my mouth before I knew what I was saying." I explain.

"So what are you going to do about it?" She asks after letting my explanation sink in.

"I'm hoping I can convince Lily to play along until Erica leaves town. Mom, you need to know she is claiming the baby is mine." I say in a rush.

"What the fuck!" She shouts.

Oh shit, my mom never swears. She was there when Erica told me I wasn't the father. I think she was more heartbroken than I was over it. She wanted to be a Grandma so badly, she claimed Hanley as her own after we moved here.

"Austin, if that baby is yours you better bring it home to Nana." I can hear her starting to cry.

"Mom. I swear to you if Cordelia is mine, she is not going anywhere." I promise.

"Cordelia? She had a girl?" Mom sniffles.

"Yes, Mama. Look, I have to go. I'm sitting in the parking lot at the grocery store. They're going to think I'm casing the joint if I sit here much longer. I've gotta get home and clean up before Lily gets off work."

"You're seeing her tonight?" She asks.

"I'm cooking dinner; if I want her to play along I have to tell her everything."

"Austin James, you said she is a friend but you are cooking for her." I hear the question in her voice.

"Yes and ..." I can just picture the twinkle in my mom's eye and hear the hope in her voice.

"Nothing at all baby, you come home and cook for your friend." She says, excitedly.

"Mom, I love you. I'm on my way now." I say quickly before hanging up.

It doesn't take me long to get ready. With just me and Mom living here, we don't make a mess. I time dinner so that it's done just before I go pick up Lily. The table is set, plates in the oven to stay warm, I give the house one more look before I head for Poison Pen.

Getting there with a few minutes to spare. Fiona is cleaning her equipment. Arin is sweeping the floor and Lily is finishing up with a client. She looks up when I walk in. I can't help but notice her smile.

"I'm almost done." She calls out, so I take a seat and watch her. It's like I'm looking at her for the first time. Her long hair is pulled back from her face in a braid that hangs over her shoulder. Her slim legs that could wrap around my body, I know those legs have enough strength to hold on tight.

I can just picture her above me riding my cock. Shit, I adjust myself hoping no one notices the boner I'm sporting. I'm lost in the fantasy when a smack to the back of my head gets my attention. Baratta is standing behind me.

"I hope that look wasn't meant for my woman." He grins.

"Nope, not at all." I assure him

"Austin I like you, but if you hurt Lily..." is all he says before he walks over to Fiona.

Look for it here:
https://books2read.com/LilysShadow

Sneak Peak of
All I've Got
Chapter 1

Becky

"I'm going to be late for work. Do you have everything in your bag?" I ask Max as we get into the car.

He never looks up from his phone, just shakes his head as if I can hear him.

"Max, I asked you a question." I patiently say.

"I answered." He huffs, having been interrupted from his perusal of his video.

"No, you didn't. Shaking your head is not an answer." I turn left onto the street that leads to his friend Tommy's house.

"Yes, mom, I got everything." He calmly answers finally while putting his phone away.

"I'll see you later when Mr. Scott drops you off at the diner."

I pull up into the Scott's driveway and watch as Mrs. Scott steps out on the porch giving me a little wave.

"Love you, Mom!" Max shouts as he jumps out, running to the porch.

I wave back at Mrs. Scott before pulling back out onto the road. Harry, my boss at the diner, is going to be a little ill about my running late but his wife, Martha, always calms him down.

He's not a bad guy really. He treats me like the daughter he and his wife never had. They were never able to have children. While they always seemed okay with that, I still get the feeling that it saddens them.

Growing up in this town was hard for me. My family didn't have money, not even to keep the lights on from month to month. Harry and Martha took me under their wing even back then. Always making sure that I had something to eat and clean clothes to wear to school. My mom never even noticed.

The year I turned sixteen is when things went from bad to worse. That's the year that Max's dad took an interest in me. Craving attention that I never received before, I soaked it up like a sponge never really knowing that all James wanted was to get in my pants. Once he had that, I no longer existed for him.

Once he found out about Max, he spread lies all over town about seeing me at the local bar just outside of town giving it up to every trucker that happened through. After going through all of that, I never told the truth about who Max's father was.

The only one I'll ever owe an explanation to is Max. When the day comes and he asks, I'll tell him the truth about all of it.

Pulling up at the diner, I park the car and head inside, slipping my apron on as I walk through the back.

"There you are. You're late! Thought we'd be short handed." Harry growls but I smile at him, kissing his cheek as I pass by. "Don't think to butter me up, missy!" Although he sounds harsh, he smiles as I go to the front to find Martha at the counter.

"There's my sweet girl! Can you go take that couple in the back order while I ring up this gentleman?" She asks in her sweet voice.

"Yes ma'am." I answer as I get to work.

Brian

Getting to the ball park where the all star team is practicing, I stay out of sight just to watch for a few minutes. This is the best way to catch things the kids may need a little work on.

One boy in particular stands out from the rest. He seems to have a natural talent for the game. As he steps up to the plate though I notice his stance is a little off. It's not a huge issue as long as it is corrected. I have the perfect solution for it in one of my bags.

It's a stance trainer. There's quite a few on the market but they truly do work. When you practice standing the correct way, eventually your body will do it automatically.

Sonny Richardson finally notices me before anyone else does. He's the reason I was invited to coach this all-star team. We've been friends since we first met in college. While my baseball career took off, he finished up law school.

About a year ago, I came down wrong on one of my knees during a game. It messed it up pretty good. Even after surgery I knew I would never be able to go back to playing the game I loved.

Sonny is the one that planted the seed into my head about teaching the game to the younger generation. Not that I needed a job or anything. I've made enough during my short career and invested it well so that I am set for life.

"I was wondering when you would get here." He says, walking up beside me.

"I've been here for a few minutes. I just wanted to watch the boys without them knowing that I'm here already. I figure they'll try too hard to impress me when I really just need to watch for anything they may need more work on." I explain, still watching the boy at the plate.

"That's actually a good idea." He laughs a little.

"Who's the kid at the plate? I noticed him as soon as I got here. He's got some natural talent." I ask with interest.

"That would be Max Ross. He's a damn fine little ball player, but I wouldn't count on him staying on the team." He comments with the shake of his head.

"Why is that?" I ask, wondering if there is a problem with the boy's home life.

"The boosters will cut anyone who can't afford the fees for the all star league. His mom works at a diner. Her name is Rebeccah but she goes by Becky. The other moms will take great delight in her not being able to afford it." He explains as we continue to watch.

"So you brought me into a vipers nest." I laugh.

"You can handle them. Personally, I hope she does get all the funds to cover his fees. Serve those bitches right. He's the best player on the team as it is, although they would try to argue that fact."

"Why not just do fundraisers to help the kids get all the money?" I ask but I am sure I already know the answer.

I know these types of people because it's what I grew up with. My family was one of the poorest in my hometown. I was ridiculed constantly at school but I absolutely dominated the baseball field.

"That would be what others would do. But if they did that, then it's possible anyone could be let on the team." He confirms my suspicion.

"People are jackasses." I growl.

"You are certainly right about these jackasses." He whispers back.

Chapter 2
Becky

About an hour into my shift a few of the women I went to school with walk in. As much as I would like to ignore them, I'm the only waitress here at the moment.

"Can I take your order?" I say as politely as I can.

"Three hamburgers with fries on the side and tea to drink. Try not to get your greasy hair in it." Karen quickly says with a sneer.

Not wanting to give her the reaction I know she is looking for, I walk away from the table to give Harry the order.

After I deliver their food, I walk around wiping down the tables trying to ignore their conversation. They do this about once a week. They'll come in here just to run their mouths hoping I'll say something back. I learned a long time ago that showing anger of any kind puts a huge smile on Karen and her friends' faces.

"She is so nasty. I really can't imagine what Mr. and Mrs. Crawly were thinking, hiring her to work here. She probably blows every new customer that comes through in the back alley." They talk loud enough for me to hear but I continue working hoping they don't stay long.

"Didn't your husband show an interest in her back in high school senior year?" Catherine asks Karen.

"Boys are allowed a few indiscretions while still young. Besides, it was well known even then that she was an easy lay. We can't expect young men to just ignore that all the time." Karen says with a confidence that even I don't believe.

"Of course not. If she was giving it away, she deserved what she got." Megan throws into the conversation not wanting to be left out.

After they finish with their food, they don't stay too much longer before leaving. I'm just thankful not too many other patrons came in while they were here although quite a few have been known to come to my defense when hearing the remarks coming from those three.

"Those three still need a good switch to their backside." Martha says as we watch them walk to their cars.

"Well if anyone decides to do the switching make sure they record it. We can post it online and become famous." We both laugh at the thought.

"Oh I was supposed to tell you that Sara Richardson was needing someone who could clean her office building on the weekends. She thought you would be perfect for the job." Martha says.

"That'll be great! I need the extra right now to cover Max's fees with the all-star team." I smile at the thought.

"Hey mom!" Max shouts, walking through the door.

"Hey kiddo. How was practice?" I ask, grabbing a quick hug. Luckily he's not yet reached the age where all public displays of my affection are off limits.

"It was awesome! The new coach that used to play for the Mets was there. He's so awesome! He took time to show me the right placement for my feet at the plate. I'm supposed to practice standing that way every day until next practice." Smiling at his enthusiasm, I guide him to a booth to sit in until my shift is over.

I go to the back to place an order for him so that he can eat. When it's ready, I pick it up and head back to his booth. When I do, I notice a man I've never seen before sitting in the booth with him. Panic rises in my chest as I hurry over.

"Hey mom, this is Coach Brian." Max says when I walk up, placing his food in front of him.

Coach Brian stands up holding his hand out to me. Taking it, I shake his hand.

"Nice to meet you Mrs..."

"Ross. It's just Miss though." I smile in greeting. "It's nice to meet you as well. Max here has been super excited about you coming to coach the all-star team."

"Yeah, working with kids is great." He smiles back, finally letting go of my hand.

"Can I get you something to eat?" I grab my order pad waiting.

After giving me his order, I get back to my job as more people come in for the dinner hour.

Brian

I sit with Max while eating dinner and easily talk baseball with him. He's not just interested in the things I have done, he truly wants to learn the ins and outs of baseball.

I watch Becky from the corner of my eye while she is busy working. The woman is absolutely gorgeous with the kindest eyes. She's probably the first one to not automatically flirt with me like the other moms did during practice.

I've actually debated making it mandatory that all parents must leave while practice is in session. If I have to put up with those women again, I'm likely to quit. Their snide remarks about Max during practice had me gritting my teeth so much that I've probably broken several.

"So, do you like school?" I ask him between bites.

"Only the classes that I don't have with Luke." He grumbles with his mouth full.

"You talking about the same Luke from the team?" I ask, my interest spiking.

He just shakes his head in answer this time instead of trying to talk around his food.

"You want to tell me why?" I whisper to him.

He looks around until he sees that his mom is behind the counter before turning back to look at me.

"You aren't going to tell my mom are you?" He says with a serious expression.

"I promise. It'll just be between us guys." Although I promise him, I know that if it's too bad I will have to tell his mom.

"He likes to call me a bastard and gets the other kids to say it too." He shrugs like it's not that big of a deal.

"I'm guessing you know what the word means?" I ask him.

"Yeah, I know what it means but I don't care. Not really. I watch the other boys at school with their dads and some of them aren't that nice. Except Mr. Scott, he never yells at Tommy or me. Even if we mess up." I listen as he explains it all from his perspective and can tell that while he's had it rough, deep down he's a smart little boy that will go far in life.

"My dad doesn't yell either. Not even when I mess up." I smile at him as we finish eating.

A little while later, I say my goodbyes to Max before walking up to the counter to pay for my tab.

"Leaving already? I hope your food was to your liking." Becky greets me at the cash register.

"It was very good actually. I'm just going to head home. The movers moved everything in but I only just got here this morning so I'm a little tired." I smile, handing her my credit card.

"Here you go." She says, handing me the card and a receipt.

"Would you like to have coffee with me sometime?" I smile hoping that she will agree. A woman hasn't turned my head in a really long time. This one, not batting her lashes at me, intrigues the hell out of me.

"I don't think that would be a very good idea." She answers, looking around as if to see if anyone heard.

"Why wouldn't it be?" I ask.

"I'm not that kind of woman. Thank you Coach Brian. Have a good night." She firmly says before walking away.

Accepting the no for now, I stick the receipt in my pocket as I head out the door. I'll get her to have coffee with me, I vow to myself. Any woman that doesn't automatically turn on her charms from looking at me is definitely worth a second look. Even a third and fourth look.

COMING SOON...

Thank you for reading my books. It means more to me than you will ever know.
Would you like to talk to me directly or know when there are openings on my ARC team? Come find me on my Facebook Reader group, Marissa Ann Romance Readers.

www.ingramcontent.com/pod-product-compliance
Lightning Source LLC
Chambersburg PA
CBHW021732190726
48288CB00009B/3011